Fast and Loose

A Novelette by David Olivieri

Edith Wharton

FAST AND LOOSE

A NOVELETTE

BY DAVID OLIVIERI

Edited with an Introduction
by Viola Hopkins Winner

University Press of Virginia

Charlottesville

THE UNIVERSITY PRESS OF VIRGINIA
Copyright © 1977 by the Rector and Visitors
of the University of Virginia

First published 1977

Frontispiece:
Edith Newbold Jones in 1876,
age fourteen. (Courtesy the Lilly Library,
Indiana University, Bloomington.)

Library of Congress Cataloging in Publication Data

Wharton, Edith Newbold Jones, 1862–1937.
Fast and loose.

I. Title
PZ3.W555Fas5   [PS3545.H16]   813'.5'2   76–58438
ISBN 0–8139–0599–0

Printed in the United States of America

Contents

Illustrations

Foreword

YOUR FRIENDSHIP WITH Edith," wrote Percy Lubbock to me in 1947, ten years after her death, "was in its way unique; for you must have been the only friend she ever had who was a friend from his birth, and a friend without break or interruption until she died."

This indeed unique friendship had its origin in a chance meeting between my father and Edith Wharton in Paris, in 1912, at the apartment of a mutual French friend. By the time World War I broke out, Royall and Elisina Tyler (who were living in Paris in an apartment on the Île Saint-Louis) and Edith Wharton were seeing a good deal of each other, and the circle of their mutual friends had grown. Early in 1915 Edith Wharton asked my mother if she would be willing to help her organize and run the charities for poor and sick war refugees, which she was founding. My mother at once agreed, becoming vice-chairman of "Les Maisons franco-américaines de Convalescence" for the rest of the war. Out of these years of intimate collaboration and joint effort grew a friendship that was never to wane between my parents and Edith Wharton. My earliest memories of her date from those years—books and toys for Christmas and my birthdays—meals with grown-ups at her apartment in the rue de Varenne, whose telephone number

(Saxe 06–13) I heard my mother call so often that I never forgot it later.

As I grew up, I became more and more fond of "Edoo," as I called her, and found more pleasure in her company than in that of any other adult. Although I spent most of my time after the war at school in England, whereas she lived in France, we never lost touch, and her influence on me became greater than that of my parents. In a letter I wrote to Percy Lubbock in 1947, after reading his *Portrait of Edith Wharton*, I tried to express the nature of my feelings for her: "I knew her before the age of reason, and as my tastes and mind developed she was always there as an influence, an attraction and a force as natural and compelling as the seasons. After her death I realized that, quite literally, I could not imagine the world without her." I went on to describe the qualities which endeared her so much to me: "In short, she was uniquely and perfectly accessible; and though I did not then always understand why she sometimes laughed at what I said, I knew that she never did so unkindly, and she never daunted me . . . she never crushed an opinion, however immature or uncongenial to her, by a show of learning or authority. She was the most buoyant human being I have ever known, or shall, doubtless, ever know. . . . Her sympathetic interest, and the plane on which it was expressed, gave me a greater sense of confidence in myself and knowledge of the world than I could have obtained from any other source, then or since. When she condemned, it was not so much explicitly as by exclusion, and I have many times since been guided by applying what I imagined would have been her criteria."

After her death came the war years, accompanied and followed by profound changes that rapidly eliminated the world Edith Wharton had known. While she was assured of a permanent niche in the history of American literature, her writings no longer interested the reading public. Her subject matter was too remote from contemporary interests and concerns to appeal, and her social and human values seemed unacceptably restricted, if not reprehensible, to a generation that had never known the world in which she had lived, and was not sympathetic to its problems.

In recent years the pendulum has been swinging back again. The period in which Edith Wharton became famous is increasingly an object of interest and study. The social customs and values of a world that had formerly seemed bereft of significance now arouse popular curiosity to the point of fascination. The success of the recently published biography of Edith Wharton by Professor R. W. B. Lewis reflects this trend. However, to my mind the greatest achievement of this notable book is the rehabilitation of the personality and human quality of Edith Wharton. It should be noted that this is the first book on Edith Wharton which can properly be called a biography. Only its author has had access to all of the existing materials and papers from which the full story of her life, and an evocation of her as a human being, could be written, and this Professor Lewis has triumphantly achieved.

In my view, justice has at last been rendered to Edith Wharton, after nearly forty years during which her image was, as I have written elsewhere, that "of a brilliant woman, at best humanly inaccessible; at worst cold, haughty, and unpleasant to those who did not measure up to her standards or her expectations." I used to be greatly saddened by this in the past, and I pondered on the reasons why someone whose memory was so dear to me, and whose goodness of heart and generosity inspired such deep love and affection to those who knew her well, should have, by and large, appeared to posterity as a hard-hearted and snobbish woman. Undoubtedly this was to a certain extent due to the fact that Edith Wharton was an expatriate in France for the last third of her life and that she did not hesitate to publish the reasons why she preferred living in France rather than in her own country. She thus became both a remote and, from the point of view of the American public, an unappealing figure. However, I have no doubt whatever that the principal factor that established her human image for the next generation was Percy Lubbock's *Portrait of Edith Wharton.* Her personal relations with Lubbock, and especially with his wife, deteriorated sharply after their marriage, and his characterization of Edith Wharton in his *Portrait* of her clearly betrays personal animosity and the intention to cast her in an unfavorable light.

Now, with Professor Lewis's book, a new portrait of Edith Wharton has been presented to the public which, I am sure, will supersede the previous stereotype and endure for all time.

I am delighted that "Fast and Loose" should now be published, "as an overdue unveiling rather than as a merciless exposure," as Mrs. Winner so sensitively puts it in her penetrating and perceptive introduction to this phenomenal little achievement.

One of Edith Wharton's most endearing qualities was her sense of humor, the delight she took in the irony of the frailties, including her own, of human nature. In "Fast and Loose" and the accompanying "reviews," two of her characteristics, one professional and the other human, already appear full-blown: first, her extraordinary craftsmanship as a writer; and second, her sense of humor, her ability to laugh at herself, never to take herself too seriously, which she retained all her life. In the very year of her death, she sent me a letter from "Linky," her Pekingese, which concludes, "The old woman was *so* pleased that you liked *Hudson River*."

W. R. T.

Introduction

THE TEXT OF Edith Wharton's first and uncompleted novel has not survived, but its opening lines and critical reception have become a part of her legend. As she recounted in her autobiography, *A Backward Glance* (1934), her first effort began with this bit of dialogue: " 'Oh, how do you do, Mrs. Brown?' said Mrs. Tompkins. 'If only I had known you were going to call I should have tidied up the drawing-room.' " The budding novelist of twelve eagerly gave it to her mother to read. She soon returned it with the "icy comment: 'Drawing-rooms are always tidy.' " This response, Mrs. Wharton recalled, was "so crushing to a would-be novelist of manners that it shook me rudely out of my dream of writing fiction, and I took to poetry instead." Fortunately, her urge to make up stories proved irrepressible, and no doubt her mother's intimidating sense of decorum was ultimately the source for her own unerring grasp of social detail.

But it was as a poet that in 1879 she made her debut in print, auspiciously, in the the *Atlantic Monthly*. How she happened to be published here offers a pleasant instance of literary continuity in American letters, for the editor was William Dean Howells, always remarkably generous to young writers. Edith Jones's poems had come to him from Longfellow with some favorable comments; he in turn had been shown them by her brother's friend Allen Thorndike Rice, afterwards editor of the *North American Review*. Probably what passed through this succession of distinguished hands was *Verses*, a selection of twenty-nine poems that had been privately printed the year before in Newport. Edith's mother, Lucretia Jones, had arranged the publication and had chosen the poems from a notebook she kept of her writings. (Her family, especially her mother, encouraged her youthful literary ambitions far more than the elderly author recognized in her autobiographical writings or in her fictional portrayals of the intellectual atmosphere of old New York.) While one can see why Longfellow might consider these poems extraordinary for having been written by a girl of sixteen "brought up in fashionable surroundings little calculated to feed her taste for the Muses," in themselves, even taking into account Victorian taste, they do not reveal unusual poetic talent. Perhaps Blake Nevius goes too far in saying that with one exception they "might have been attributed to any literary young lady anywhere," but he is right in finding they lack "the authentic personal note."

Despite its mawkishness and other girlish excesses, this note abounds in her second try at a novel, begun in the autumn of 1876 and finished in early January 1877. Unlike her juvenile verse, *Fast and Loose, a Novelette*, was not written to be circulated even in the family but rather, again according to *A Backward Glance*, was "destined for the private enjoyment of a girl friend and never exposed to the garish light of print." It is especially appropriate, therefore, that it should make its entrance into the wider world discreetly in this limited edition. Its publication, in any event, should be viewed as an overdue unveiling rather than as a merciless exposure, for it is a remarkable achievement for an author not yet fifteen. For its flashes of originality and ingenuous charm it stands alone; for its intimations of her mature style and habits of mind it is a vestibule to her fiction well worth visiting.

Fast and Loose had a special meaning to Edith Wharton; it was not only an expression of her youthful wit but an occasion for it. Long before her wryly disparaging comments on it in *A Backward Glance*, she had measured it and found it wanting. The history of her self-criticism begins with the sprightly mock reviews that appear in print for the first time here. Written shortly after the novella, these reviews, supposedly from the *Saturday Review*, the *Pall Mall Budget*, and the *Nation*, severely chastise the author for schoolgirlish tameness and artistic ineptness. Revealing an unusual sophistication and detachment, she is harder on herself than a truly dispassionate critic, taking into consideration her age, would be. Happily, she turned her disappointed realization of her failure to fulfill her intentions into a comic performance in which shrewd insights into her deficiencies are presented with sparkle and verve. Her world-weary, waspish tone amusingly parodies the style of American and English reviewers of the day.

Subsequently, in stories more than twenty years later when she was on her way to becoming a professional writer, she made of her novelette and of *Lucile,* the verse novel from which her title derives, a kind of running joke. She must have reread her juvenilia at this time, a decisive period in her creative life. By "Owen Meredith" (the pseudonym of the popular British writer Robert Lytton), *Lucile* was a staple ornament of the Victorian parlor table and a book she herself had obviously enjoyed. It is referred to in an early story, "The

Muse's Tragedy" (1899), to indicate an uncultivated taste: the "perfectly beautiful" but unintelligent young woman (her mind is "all elbows") gives it to the great poet Rendle as a birthday present. In "April Showers" (1900), the last lines of *Fast and Loose* are quoted as the ending of the first novel of the seventeen-year-old Theodora, who is "almost sure" that she has written "a remarkable book," its "emotional intensity" compensating for its lack of "lightness of touch." This novel, Theodora hopes, will bring her fame and money, and freedom from a burdensome household in which her mother is an invalid and her father unprosperous—mirroring, perhaps, Edith Jones's dreams of a literary career and also perhaps the desire to be free of her family. Still another and more explicit reference occurs in the amusing story "Expiation" (1904), in which the aspiring author, Mrs. Fetheral, tries to launch her career with what she believes to be a daring novel exposing "the hollowness of social conventions." It fails to live up to its racy title, *Fast and Loose*, but becomes a *succès de scandale* after being denounced from the pulpit by the Bishop of Ossining.

Despite Edith Wharton's playful deflation of *Fast and Loose*, a private joke on herself, the devotion of this much attention to an adolescent friendship offering suggests a greater commitment to it and hopes for it than she admitted. Her cool intelligence alone distinguishes her from the deluded Theodora and rather silly Mrs. Fetheral, but at least momentarily one suspects she shared their delusions. Her persistent artistic self-doubt would further account for these probings. It was a characteristic of Edith Wharton to fictionalize her emotions and experiences without realizing the extent to which she was being self-revelatory.

In his admirable and indispensable biography of Edith Wharton, R. W. B. Lewis briefly connects the life with the art in his parenthetic observation that her vision, incipient in this novella, "of human aspiration doomed to defeat almost by its very nature" was "based primarily upon her observation of her parents' life together." There are, of course, other biographical connections that could be made if we were to read the story as a psychological paradigm: for instance, Georgie's mother is described as a "nervous invalid, of the complainingly resigned sort." She is a widow who has lost not only her husband but all traces of beauty she may have ever had. In the light of what we know about Edith's relationship with her deceptively self-effacing mother, whom she did not like, and her father, whom she did, this portrayal is too blatant as a wish-fulfilling dream to require comment. It is more interesting to speculate on Edith's portrayal of herself in Georgie: one may trace in Georgie—her tomboyishness and affected masculinity, which piquantly accentuate her plump, peaches-and-cream feminity—Edith's divided self. On the one hand, she too wanted to be devastatingly attractive to men and, on the other, to be as free as a man to pursue a literary career. It would be preposterous to view Edith Jones's marriage to the somewhat older Edward Wharton as an ironic reenactment of Georgie's fatally incompatible marriage to the ancient Lord Breton, but it is striking that Georgie is not allowed to marry, as she describes him, "the only man I ever knew who neither despises me nor is afraid of me." One guesses that scorn or fear of her was what the intellectually formidable Edith Jones thought young men felt about *her*. Perhaps one of the reasons she married Edward Wharton was that, like Breton for Georgie, he did not pose the threat to self-assertion and independence that marriage to an equal in mind and spirit might have presented.

Fast and Loose is also more generally and superficially self-revelatory. Edith probably had, as she said of herself jokingly in a review, begun by trying "to make it as bad as Wilhelm Meister, Consuelo, & 'Goodbye Sweetheart' " altogether. For "bad" we should read full of passionate love and defiance of social convention. She was not exempt from the usual adolescent impulse to *épater* her elders and dazzle her contemporaries. Finally, though, as this first work is literary rather than confessional in flavor and inspiration, what it tells us about her intellectual development and predilections takes precedence over its psychological import. A sentimental novel of manners, it is the antithesis of the autobiographical, the type based on actual experiences she attributed to the writer Vance Weston in *Hudson River Bracketed* (1929).

Her reading of *Wilhelm Meister* by fifteen (there is other evidence that she had, and *Faust* as well) shows not only a superior command of German, but as one critic has put it, "tenacity or at least patience." *Wilhelm Meister* was heavy going even for the intellectuals among her elders. *Consuelo* required of her no special linguistic effort, as she read French fluently; it is even possible that she may have learned to read French before English. She knew Italian well, perhaps more colloquially than literarily. Her pseudonym, "David Olivieri," and the sprinkling throughout the text of French and Italian phrases testify to her cosmopolitan upbringing. Most of her childhood, from the ages of four to ten, the Jones family lived abroad, in Paris and Rome, traveling in Germany and Spain as well. American writing hardly entered her consciousness until relatively late in life, except for those genteel authors in her father's library like Washington Irving and Fitz-Greene Halleck. Thus there is no American predecessor haunting her apprentice fiction in form or tone, as Hawthorne did James. (In itself this novella disproves the lingering popular myth that she was Henry James's disciple; she had clearly discovered her own voice long before meeting or reading him.) There are Americanisms, to be sure; occasional idioms as when Egerton compares involvement with a woman to picking up a rattlesnake; an overattention to social rank, such as calling a guardsman a "Duke's son"—an English writer would be less socially self-conscious. Most glaring, perhaps, is the repeated habit of referring to characters as "English," for example, to Mr. Graham as an "English merchant" when presumably the story is narrated from an English perspective. That Edith Jones should have chosen English characters placed in English and continental settings for her novel may be its most American characteristic: where else but in Europe could one imagine a young woman torn between love and a title, a brilliant social career, great wealth? At any rate, at this stage in her life, Edith Wharton clearly identified "literature" with the Old World.

As the epigraphs, literary echoes, and allusions indicate, her taste was fairly traditional for the time: in poetry, chiefly Tennyson, Browning, and Scott; in fiction, Thackeray, Trollope, and Jane Austen. There are some obvious borrowings: Georgie's valetudinarian mother resembles Emma's father. In answer to Georgie's question whether the maid was likely to enter, she replies, " 'Indeed I can't tell, my dear.' (Mrs. Rivers was never in her life known to express a positive opinion on any subject.)." When Georgie, about to reveal that she is changing fiancés, warns her, " 'Now, Mamma, I am going to shock you,' " her reply is true to type: " 'Oh, my dear, I hope not.' " Georgie's relation to Lord Breton is like that of Lady Teasdale's to her husband, though Lord Breton calls to mind the superannuated Restoration rake or Regency buck rather than the disguised man of feeling. Courting Georgie, he conjures up "the ghost of what some might recall as a fascinating smile; but which was more like a bland leer to the eye unassisted by memory." Georgie is compared to Beatrix Esmond, and some of the characters, in name at least, are straight from the pages of Trollope: Miss Priggett, the maid; Dr. Ashley Patchem; Doublequick, the guardsman. Her crisp, epigrammatic style may be traced to eighteenth-century prose, as her sentences, which formally balance thesis and antithesis, suggest: "Meanwhile, he had enjoyed himself, made love to her, & lived neither better nor worse than a hundred other young men of that large class delightful for acquaintance, but dangerous for matrimony, whom susceptible young ladies call 'fascinating' & anxious mothers 'fast.' "

Edith Jones's reading in her teens was not as austerely confined to the great classics as she later remembered in *A Backward Glance*. Either she was less dutiful or her mother, who forbade her to read popular fiction, including Rhoda Broughton and "all the lesser novelists of the day," was less strict than memory served, for she not only read Broughton's *"Goodbye-Sweetheart!"* and *Lucile*, by Robert Lytton, a lesser novelist if anyone was, but paid them the compliment of imitation in *Fast and Loose.* She showed instinctive good sense in modeling herself on these relatively short and simplistic works, instead of, for instance, Goethe's philosophical Bildungsroman, Sand's picaresque romance, or Thackeray's densely populated novel without a hero. While the scaling down of artistic ends to the means may preclude the creation of sublime masterpieces, it gets the work done and the craft learned.

Rhoda Broughton (1840–1920), speaking of her own reputation, is said to have quipped that she began her career as Zola and was ending it as Miss Yonge. Now she is chiefly known as Henry James's great good friend; Edith Wharton's path probably crossed hers more than once when she made her periodic swoops on London in later life. Actually, while it is not Zola, Broughton's novel is not the insipid Victorian lady's book of the Yonge type either. Its second half is a shambles and the heroine's death by consumption is as arbitrary as Georgie's, except that it drags on longer, but initially Lucy, the heroine, is the antitype of the blond, submissive domestic angel of convention in her physical robustness, outspokenness, even sensuality, and the smell, look, and taste of things are palpably presented. From this book Edith Jones derived hints for the characterization of Georgie as capricious, self-willed, flirtatious. She also adopted Mrs. Broughton's shorthand method of setting the scene with a series of visual details set forth like stage directions. The predominance of dialogue over narrative passages—a practice Edith Wharton was to deplore in *The Writing of Fiction*—probably also set her an example.

Before turning tragic, Mrs. Broughton introduced into her narrative realistic touches serving a mock-romantic purpose:

the lovers set out from an inn where the smell of manure has permeated even the tea. Robert Lytton's *Lucile* is high-toned throughout. The characters are mere counters in a wonderfully melodramatic plot: assignations by a waterfall in a wild landscape, duels and seductions (though unconsummated), a broken engagement, compromising letters, bankruptcy, the Crimean war, the hero's wounded son nursed by Soeur Seraphine (formerly Lucile, once the toast of Paris, Luchon, wherever she goes). Disquisitions on Life, Time, and Sorrow make up the mortar patching it all together. All very profound and no doubt in its sexual suggestiveness, urbanity, and triumphant idealism very satisfying to even a bookishly sophisticated adolescent. Though Edith Jones found much in this verse novel that appealed to her, as indicated by parallels in plot and character types as well as by quotations, she refrained from imitating its incidents of romantic adventure and its gothic touches. Moreover, she adopted an ironic narrative tone that undercuts a good deal of the sentimentality. The tears that fall in the Guy-Madeline proposal scene would make a pool to rival the one in *Alice in Wonderland*, but on another occasion, so that we do not feel too sorry for Georgie when she takes to weeping, she is described as crying her eyes "into the proper shade of pinkness." A satiric sententiousness, not entirely controlled or consistent, replaces Lytton's philosophizing. We never quite see how Guy goes "rapidly to the dogs," but the direction is clearly for the author towards psychological realism:

Now there are many modes of travelling on this road; the melodramatic one in which the dark-browed hero takes to murder, elopement, & sedition; the commonplace one in which drinking, gambling & duelling are prominent features; the precipitate one of suicide; & finally that one which Guy himself had chosen. He did not kill himself, as we have seen, nor did he run away with anyone, or fight a duel, or drink hard; but he seemed to grow careless of life, money & health, & to lose whatever faith & tenderness he had had in a sort of undefined skepticism.

Lucile abounds in the rhetoric of disappointed love; in *Fast and Loose* (see p. 27) this rhetoric is mocked and we are rather elaborately spared the clichés. Worldly wisdom in general is dispensed briskly and brightly: though "the wife is a legitimate object of wrath, it is wise to restrain one's self during courtship"; or, Lord Breton was "charmed by this pretty display of wilfulness (as men are apt to be before marriage)." Of course lines such as these gain an extraliterary lift as a wise child's sayings. But what sounds here is the satiric note that became what James called Edith Wharton's "fine asperity," that finely turned phrase, sometimes with a cutting edge, that characterized her maturity. If one can be said to have lisped satirically, Edith Wharton did.

The author's relation to his characters also anticipates the mature writer; the authorial voice audibly mediates between the reader and the characters much as it does in Thackeray's and Trollope's pronouncements on motives and behavior. Although there are a few works, most strikingly *The Reef*, in which Mrs. Wharton adopted a Jamesian practice in controlling point of view and exploring a situation in psychological or moral depth, her typical works are what she herself called "chronicle novels," in which point of view indiscriminately shifts or is omniscient, and the author comments overtly on character and on social, philosophical issues. It is striking the degree to which in *Fast and Loose* she discovered her tone and approach. She perfected her craft but fundamentally did not expand its circumference.

Thematically, in the depiction of the heroine's plight and the final separation of the lovers, *Fast and Loose* also foreshadows the later work. Georgie, after choosing the "world" in the form of Lord Breton instead of "love," is the ancestress of numerous sensitive, intelligent "free spirits" trapped in a confining relationship—Lily Bart, Ralph Marvell, Ethan Frome, Newland Archer, Nan St. George, to name a few in the better-known works. While the sad ending is pro forma, the particular working out of the effects of Georgie's decision is a personal expression of the author's and suggests that her mature pessimism—that view of life embodied in the Eumenides haunting Lily Bart—ratified by deterministic thought and deepened by adult experience, was almost innate. The instances of irony of fate in her work are numerous and usually at the end: Seldon's going to Lily to declare his love just after she has died from an overdose of chloral, the discovery that the querulous voice in Frome's kitchen is Mattie Silver's; Undine's realization that, having climbed the social ladder through divorce, she can never fulfill her "ultimate" ambition to be the wife of an ambassador because an ambassadress cannot have been divorced. The short stories frequently turn on a reversal of this kind—sometimes amusing ("The Pelican"), sometimes cruel ("Roman Fever"). In *Fast and Loose* the inscrutable, often punitive force governing human lives is manifested to begin with in Mrs. Graham's accident: "It is certain that in this world the smallest wires work the largest machinery in a wonderful way." If it had not been for this twist of her foot on the stairs Guy would probably not have become engaged to Madeline (or so we are supposed to believe). Thus, after Lord Breton dies and Georgie is free, Guy is not. Then Georgie dies but Guy remains forever true to her, in his heart. By another twist of fate, Teresina, who in contrast to Georgie has married the poor young lover instead of the rich old suitor, is deserted by her husband. She is rescued by Madeline and Guy, but the husband never returns. So much for a marriage of true minds. The marriage of the misogynistic Jack Egerton to a "pale, melancholy, fascinating French Marquise" is a last ironic touch.

The male characters in Edith Wharton's fiction tend to be opposites: on the one hand, the man of power—brash, socially ambitious, plebian or plutocratic—and on the other, the man of refined sensibilities—artistic, aristocratic, too morally sensitive to succeed in a materialistic society. Though Graham is not a rival, the initial antagonism between Guy and Graham calls to mind the pairing of other opposites: Simon Rosedale and Lawrence Seldon, Elmer Moffatt and Ralph Marvell, Julius Beaufort and Newland Archer, Bunty Hayes and Vance Weston. Moreover, Graham, like the later "new" men, is shown in a more kindly light as the work progresses. At first he is a pompous fool and comic butt; although his judgment in art remains primitive, he becomes likable and an exemplary father-in-law. Likewise, for instance, for more complex and artistically explicable reasons, Moffatt enlists our sympathy and respect by the end and Simon Rosedale and Bunty Hayes are similarly humanized. The explanation for this transformation of caricature into sympathetic character has something to do with Edith Wharton's relation to her other, much more prevalent male type, the "gentleman." Most of her "heroes," including John Amherst in *The Fruits of the Tree* (1907) and

Odo in *The Valley of Decision* (1902), are cut from the same cloth, and rather blandly colored at that. Although her treatment of them is certainly at times negatively ambiguous—especially of Seldon and Darrow—she gave her allegiance to them because they represented "civilization," the life of the mind. Her underground attraction to the entrepreneur or man of action may be accounted for by what she felt was missing in the men of her own class—energy, power, will, passion.

Georgie's vividness as a character is certainly not enough to put her in a class with Edith Wharton's truly memorable women, but beginning with *Fast and Loose* the heroines tend to be more successful character creations than their masculine counterparts. They are portrayed as complex beings who, even when essentially passive, like Lily or Sophy, are sensitive *and* vital; they are endowed with the energies and passions Mrs. Wharton usually attributed to her unreflective male types, the Moffatts and Beauforts, as well as with the refined sensibilities of the other.

As an exercise in the craft of fiction, *Fast and Loose* shows considerable technical skill and, in its revisions, the young writer's awareness of special problems. Each chapter has organic unity yet advances the action. Too much happens, however, overall to be believable in the given span of time: enough time elapses for Georgie to be disillusioned with her marriage but not enough for Guy's disintegration. After two months the announcement that the young man's life has been ruined forever seems premature. The repeated tinkering with dates and times (see Appendix II, pp. 131–36) did not solve the problem in this work but is a favorable sign: at least she knew that it takes more than telling to create the illusion of the flow of time.

Other revisions significantly improve concreteness and visualness. She was beginning to learn how to look and to interpret her visual impressions. Her early European experience had shaped her sense of the beautiful, and the Ruskin she read in her father's library in New York woke in her the habit of precise observation. From her mother Edith inherited an eye for dress highly useful to the novelist of manners, as demonstrated, for instance, in the description of Madeline setting out in a "gray walking dress, with a quantity of light blue veil floating about her leghorn hat & looped around her throat," which is both precisely observed and characterizing. The cool, neutral, and harmonious colors and the ethereal veil give the desired impression of her madonnalike purity and reserve. The description of the English scene is merely sketched in with a few place names and patches of local color that could have been copied from Trollope alone, but the studio world of Rome and the pastoral atmosphere of Switzerland that Edith knew at first hand is more evocatively rendered. In addition to a frequently smooth interweaving of description, dialogue, and narrative summary, occasionally visual details and gestures are used with some sublety: feeling remorseful for having cast off Guy, Georgie catches a glimpse of herself in the pier glass. Her spirits revive; the sight of her adorable self in a riding habit consoles her and strengthens her resolve to marry Lord Breton despite her affection for Guy. Abstaining from comment, the author lets the mirror episode reveal by itself Georgie's ingenuous vanity and her motives for deciding to marry a rich man who will materially sustain this image of herself. Another example is the use of the handshake to mark the stages of growing intimacy between Guy and Madeline. Madeline is not socially placed, and Mrs. Graham is more the Midwestern Mom than a middle-class Englishwoman, but Edith Jones was already aware of how manners can be used fictionally to express deeper meanings. Thus, in chapter nine, she deleted the phrase "half holding out her hand," referring to Madeline, when she and Guy part just after their first meeting. This deletion makes the two handshakes that follow immediately after Mrs. Graham's accident more effective as signs of the leap forward in Guy's and Madeline's interest in each other. A very minor point indeed, but then so is the etiquette involved in Emma's unkindness to Miss Bates at Box-Hill or in May's farewell dinner for Ellen Olenska.

It is aesthetically satisfying that Edith Wharton returned to the English setting and the dilemmas of mismarriage of *Fast and Loose* in her last—unfortunately unfinished—novel, *The Buccaneers* (1938). Its period is that of her youth in the 1870s, impressionistically recreated, rather than described, with shimmering sensuousness. The unhappily separated lovers, Nan St. George and Guy Thwarte, echo in name and plight Georgie and Guy Hastings. However, according to Mrs. Wharton's scenario, they were to find happiness together, unlike Guy and Georgie, whose reconciliation comes "too late." Despite this difference and the others that distinguish the artist from the apprentice, the resemblances exemplify finally the striking extent to which this novella anticipates her maturity. On the other hand, I cannot think of a subsequent work that has the naive élan and buoyancy, even in its most lugubrious passages, of *Fast and Loose*.

The lively interest of Clifton Waller Barrett and William R.

Tyler has been vital to the publication of this book. We are also indebted to R. W. B. Lewis, to the Associates of the Library of the University of Virginia for their support, and to Yale University for permission to quote from the manuscript of Edith Wharton's "Life and I," in the Edith Wharton Papers in the Collection of American Literature, The Beinecke Rare Book and Manuscript Library, Yale University.

V. H. W.

A Note on the Text

THE TEXT FOR this edition is the manuscript in the Clifton Waller Barrett Collection of the University of Virginia Library. The manuscript is in ink and in a finely formed Spencerian handwriting, the hallmark of feminine gentility of the period. It takes up 119 pages, mistakenly misnumbered 129, of lined paper in a notebook 6½ inches by 8½ inches. The numbering error occurs at page 89, the verso of which is numbered 100; the numbering continues in sequence from there. "Fast and Loose, A Novelette by David Olivieri" appears both on the first page, in the author's handwriting, and on a Bristol board label the size of a visiting card affixed to the cover, probably in the author's lettering. The quotation and dedication are on the inside cover. It is one of the oddities of this manuscript that, as reproduced here, the table of contents has been placed at the end of the text. The concluding inscription—"Begun in the Autumn of 1876 at Pencraig, Newport; finished January 7th 1877 at New York"—is in the more fluent and expansive handwriting of Edith Wharton's maturity. The manuscript is mostly a clean copy; the revisions in the original handwriting suggest that this was a final copy of a previous draft. Some pages have been removed but without loss of text. The manuscript of the reviews, now in the Wharton Manuscripts, Lilly Library, Indiana University, Bloomington, in the same handwriting as the text and also in ink, consists of loose sheets, one for each review. They were kept with letters, clippings, and sundry documents of Edith Wharton's youth in the same lot of material as the manuscript of *Fast and Loose.*

To keep the flavor of Edith Wharton's youthful style, I have followed her revised text in paragraphing, punctuation, capitalization, and spelling. A printed text reproducing all her idiosyncracies would be, however, virtually unreadable, and a misrepresentation of her intentions, for the hand-written draft is not a manuscript prepared for publication. Her dashes present the main problem: although sometimes used conventionally for emphasis or interrupted speech, they not only vary in length from little more than an extended period to half a line but often appear inexpressively beneath, or instead of, other forms of punctuation (see facsimile).

Concluding that literal transcription would be impracticable and at best faithful only to her handwriting, I have made conventional substitutions or deletions where the dashes seemed to me clearly unintended. I have also silently corrected a few obvious mechanical errors, such as missing commas or quotation marks, using as my guide her own practice elsewhere in the text. For a few other matters I have followed the practice of her first published book of fiction, *The Greater Inclination*: I have normalized titles appearing in the original as "Mr.," "Mrs.," and "Dr." with the *r* or *rs* raised and underlined; such words as *anybody, everybody,* and *anybody,* written unconventionally as two words, are spelled normally; the use of many dots to indicate ellipsis (see facsimile) has been modernized.

Modern practice has also been followed in the handling of correspondence within the text in that letters run in, in the manuscript, are printed here in extract form. In the placing of quotation marks with a dash to represent interrupted speech, the author's "— appears here as —."

Lists of misspelled words and of the author's stylistic revisions are appended. Not listed are the author's changes or corrections that I take to be not stylistic but purely mechanical.

V. H. W.

Fast and Loose.
A Novelette.
By
David Olivieri.

... "Let woman beware
How she plays fast & loose thus with human despair
And the storm in man's heart." *Robert Lytton*: Lucile.

Dedication

To

Cornélie

"[Donna] beata e bella" [*illegible*] Quinta.
(October 1876)

Fast and Loose—A Novelette

By David Olivieri

Chap. I. Hearts & Diamonds.

" 'Tis best to be off with the old love
Before you are on with the new!" *Song.*

A DISMAL AUTUMN AFTERNOON in the country. Without, a soft drizzle falling on yellow leaves & damp ground; within, two people playing chess by the window of the fire-lighted drawing-room at Holly Lodge. Now, when two people play chess on a rainy afternoon, tête-à-tête in a room with the door shut, they are likely to be either very much bored, or rather dangerously interested; & in this case, with all respect to romance, they appeared overcome by the profoundest ennui. The lady—a girl of about 18, plump & soft as a partridge, with vivacious brown eyes, & a cheek like a sun-warmed peach—occasionally stifled a yawn, as her antagonist, curling a slight blonde moustache (the usual sign of masculine perplexity) sat absently meditating a move on which the game, in his eyes, appeared to depend; & at last, pushing aside her chair, she rose & stood looking out of the window, as though even the dreary Autumn prospect had more attraction for her than the handsome face on the other side of the chess-board. Her movement seemed to shake her companion out of his reverie, for he rose also, & looking over her shoulder, at the soft, misty rain, observed rather languidly, "Cheerful weather!" "Horrid!" said the girl, stamping her foot. "I am dying of stagnation." "Don't

you mean to finish the game?" "If you choose. I don't care."
"Nor I—It's decidedly a bore." No answer. The bright brown
eyes & the lazy blue ones stared out of the window for the space
of five slow minutes. Then the girl said: "Guy!" "My liege!"
"You're not very amusing this afternoon." "Neither are you,
my own!" "Gallant for a lover!" she cried, pouting & turning
away from the window. "How can I amuse a stone wall? I
might talk all day!" She had a way of tossing her pretty little
head, & drawing her soft white forehead, that was quite irresistible. Guy, as the most natural thing in the world, put his
arm about her, but was met with a sharp, "Don't! You know
I hate to be taken hold of, Sir! Oh, I shall die of ennui if this
weather holds." Guy whistled, & went to lean against the fire-
place; while his betrothed stood in the middle of the room, the
very picture of "I-won't-be-amused" crossness. "Delightful!"
she said, presently. "Really, your conversation today displays
your wit & genius to a remarkable degree." "If I talk to you,
you scold, Georgie," said the lover, pathetically. "No, I don't!
I only scold when you twist your arms around me." "I can't
do one without the other!" Georgie laughed. "You *do* say nice
things, Guy! But you're a bore this afternoon, nevertheless."
"Isn't everything a bore?" "I believe so. Oh, I should be
another person gallopping over the downs on Rochester!
'What's his name is himself again!' *Shall* we be able to hunt
tomorrow?" "Ask the clerk of the weather," said Guy, rather
dismally. "Guy! I do believe you're going to sleep! Doesn't it
rouse you to think of a tear 'cross country after the hounds?
Oh, Guy, a red coat makes my blood run faster!" "Does it?—
Georgie, have you got 'Je l'ai perdu'—the thing I sent you from
London?" "Yes—somewhere." "I am going to sing," said Guy.

4

"What a treat!" "As you don't object to my smoking, I thought you mightn't mind my singing." "Well," said Georgie, mischievously, "I don't suppose it *does* matter much which sense is offended. What are you going to sing?" Guy, without answering, began to hunt through a pile of music, & at last laid a copy of "The ballad to Celia" on the piano-rack. Georgie sat down, & while he leaned against the piano, struck a few prelude-chords; then he began to sing in a rich barytone, Ben Jonson's sweet old lines. At the end of the first stanza, Georgie shut the piano with a bang. "I will not play if you sing so detestably out of time, tune & everything. Do make yourself disagreeable in some less noisy way." "I think I shall make myself agreeable—by saying goodbye." "Very well, do!" "Georgie—what is the matter?" He took her little hand as he spoke, but she wrenched it away, stamping her foot again. "Dont & dont & dont! I'm as cross as I can be & I *won't* make friends!" she cried in a sort of childish passion, running away from him to the other end of the room. He stood for a moment, twirling his moustache; then, taking up his hat, said, "Goodbye." "Goodbye—Are you *very* angry?" she said, coming a step or two nearer, & looking up through her soft lashes. "No, I suppose not. I believe I have been boring you confoundedly." "I suppose I have been very cross." "Not more than I deserved, probably. I am going to London for a few days. Will you give me your hand for goodbye?" She stood still a moment, looking at him thoughtfully; then put out her hand. "Ah, Guy, I am a worthless little thing," she said, softly, as he took it. It was her left hand & a ring set with diamonds twinkled on it. "Worth all the world to me!" he answered; then lifted the hand to his lips & turned away. As his receding steps sounded

5

through the hall, Georgie Rivers, taking a screen from the mantel-piece, sat down on the rug before the fire, with a thoughtful face out of which all the sauciness had vanished. As she watched the fire-light play on her ring, she began to think half-aloud as her childish fashion was; but Guy was cantering along the high road to West Adamsborough, & if there had been anyone to tell him what she said, he would [have] laughed—& [have] doubted it. As there was no one, however, Georgie kept her meditations to herself. "I know he thinks me a coquette," she whispered, leaning her head against her hand, "& he thinks I like to trifle with him—perhaps he is angry—(he looks very handsome when he is angry) but he doesn't know—how should he?—that I mean to break it off. I ought to have done it today, & I might have ended that beginning of a quarrel by giving him back the ring; but, oh dear, I wish—I wish I didn't care for him quite so much. He is so cool & handsome! And he is the only man I ever knew who neither despises me nor is afraid of me. Oh, Georgie, Georgie, you miserable little fool! I didn't mean to let him kiss my hand; he surprised me into it, just as he surprised me into accepting him. He always puts me off my guard, somehow! But it must be done. Perhaps I *am* in love with him, but I hope I haven't quite lost my common sense. It *must* be done, I say! I declare, I shall make an utter goose of myself in a minute! Where's that letter?" She put her hand into her pocket, & brought out an envelope, pompously sealed with a large coat of arms & motto; &, drawing out the folded sheet which it contained, slowly read aloud these words, written in a crabbed, old-fashioned hand:

6

My dear Miss Rivers: Ever since I was honoured by an introduction to you, my admiration for your charms & accomplishments has increased; & I have been sufficiently marked by your favour to hope that what I am about to say may not seem an entirely unwarrantable liberty. Although we are separated by many years, I do not perceive why that should be an obstacle to a happy union; & I therefore venture to beg that, if the profoundest admiration & respect can awaken responsive sentiments in your own bosom, you will honour me with your hand. I shall await with impatience your reply to my proposals, & am, my dear Miss Rivers, with deep esteem, Your faithful Servant

"Breton."

Georgie folded the letter again, & went on with her reflections in this wise. "I suppose I should have let him know that I was engaged to Guy, but it was so jolly to have an old Lord dangling about one, head over ears in love, &, figuratively speaking, going down on his noble, gouty knees every time one came into the room. And I really didn't think it would come to a climax so soon! I marked him by my favour, did I? And the poor old creature has got tipsy, like an old blue-bottle on a little drop of syrup. He is really in love with me! Me, Georgie Rivers, a wicked, fast, flirtatious little pauper—a lazy, luxurious coquette! Oh, Guy, Guy!—I mean, Oh, Lord Breton, Lord —ha? what's the matter?" For something dropped close by Georgie's ring, that sparkled as clearly in the fire-light as its own diamonds. "Crying! Crying! I thought I had no heart. I have always been told so. Ah, the horrid thing." She brushed the bright thing that was not a diamond away, but just then her eyes brimmed over with two more, & she was obliged to dry them with her pocket handkerchief, talking on all the while. "This is too ridiculous. Georgie getting sentimental! Georgie booh-hoohing over a lover, when she's got a real, live Lord, with a deer-park, & a house in London & ever so much a year, at her feet! What else have I always wished for? But, come, I will think of it calmly. Say I am in love with Guy (if I have no heart, how can I love anybody?) say I am in love with him. He is poor, rather extravagant, lazy & just as luxurious as I am. Now, what should we live on? I should have to mend my clothes, & do the shopping, & I should never ride or dance or do anything worth living for any more; but there would be pinching & patching & starvation (politely called economy) & I should get cross, & Guy would get cross, & we should fight, fight, fight! Now—take the other side of the picture. First, Lord B. is really in love with me. Second, he is venerable, sleepy & fixed in his own ruts, & would give me twice as much liberty as a younger man; third, I should have three fine houses, plenty of horses & as many dresses as I could wear, (& I have a large capacity in that way!) & nothing to do but coquet with all the handsome boys whose heads I chose to turn; fourth, I should be Lady Breton of Lowood, & the first lady in the county! Hurrah!" As Georgie ended this resumé of the advantages of her ancient suitor, she clapped her hands together & jumped up from the hearth-rug. "It must be done. I am sure Guy & I could never be happy together, & I shall write & tell him so, the sooner the better. I suppose Mamma will be a little scandalized, but I can settle that. And when shall I ever have such a chance again?" She reopened Lord Breton's letter, read it for the third time, & then went up to the writing table that stood between the two windows. "The sooner the better, the sooner the better," she repeated, as she sat down & took out a sheet of paper stamped with the Rivers crest. She dipped her pen in ink, dated the blank sheet—& then paused a moment, with contracting eye-brows. "No. I suppose that I must write to Guy first. What shall I say? It is so hard . . . I . . . hush, you little idiot! Are you going to change your mind again?" With this self-addressed rebuke, she re-dipped her pen, & began to write hastily—

Dear Guy: I am sure we can never be happy as anything but friends, & I send you back the ring which will be far better on someone else's hand. You will get over your fancy, & I shall Always be, Your Affectionate Cousin G.R.

To Guy Hastings Esqr.

It was soon over, & she laid the pen down & pushed the paper away quickly, covering her eyes with her hand. The clock, striking the hour on the chimney-piece, roused her with a start. "I suppose I had better take this ring off," she said, slowly, gazing at the hoop of diamonds. "There is no use in hesitating—or the battle is lost. There—what is it, a ring? It will be replaced by another (with bigger diamonds) tomorrow afternoon." She drew it off hurriedly, as though the operation were painful, & then looked at her unadorned hand. "You change owners, poor little hand!" she said softly. Then she kissed the ring & laid it away. After that it was easier to go on with her next note, though she wrote two copies before she was satisfied that it was proper to be sent to the great Lord Breton. The note finally ran thus:

*My dear Lord Breton: I was much flattered by your offer,
which I accept, remaining Yours truly
(I shall be at home tomorrow afternoon.) Georgina Rivers.*

"Like answering a dinner-invitation," commented Georgie;
"but I can't make it longer. I don't know what to say!"

Chap. II. Enter Lord Breton.

"Auld Robin Gray cam 'a courtin' me." *Lady Barnard.*

LET IT BE UNDERSTOOD by the reader, in justice to Miss Rivers, that, before she despatched the note with which our last chapter closes, she shewed it to her mother. As she had expected, that lady offered some feeble opposition to her daughter's bold stroke. It was early the next morning & Mrs. Rivers—a nervous invalid, of the complainingly resigned sort —was still in her bedroom, though the younger members of the family, Kate, Julia & Tom, had breakfasted & been called to their lessons, by Miss Blackstone, their governess. Georgie therefore found her mother alone, when she entered with the answer to Lord Breton's letter in her hand; & it was easy, after one glance at the small figure on the couch, with faded hair, pink lids & yielding wrinkles about the mouth, to see why, though "Mamma would be a little scandalized" it would be easy to "settle that." If Mrs. Rivers had ever been a beauty much mourning & malady had effaced all traces thereof from her gentle, sallow face framed in a heavy widow's cap; she was one of those meek, shrinking women who seem always overwhelmed by their clothes, & indeed by circumstances in general. She greeted her daughter's entrance with a faint smile, & observed in a thin, timid voice "that it was a beautiful morning." "Yes," said Georgie, kissing her, "jolly for hunting. How did you sleep, little Mamma?" "Oh, well enough, my dear—as well as I could have hoped," said Mrs. Rivers, sighing. "Of course Peters forgot my sleeping-draught when he went into West Adamsborough yesterday, but what else could I expect?" "I am very sorry! The man never had his proper allowance of brains." "Nay, my dear, I do not complain." "But I do," said Georgie, impatiently. "I hate to be resigned!" "My child!" "You know I do, Mamma. But I want to speak to you now. Will Payson be coming in for anything?" "Indeed I can't tell, my dear." (Mrs. Rivers was never in her life known to express a positive opinion on any subject.) "Very well, then" said Georgie, "I will make sure." She locked the door, & then came & sat down at her mother's feet. "Now, Mamma, I am going to shock you," she said. "Oh, my dear, I hope not." "But I tell you that I am," persisted Georgie. "Now listen. I have decided that I shouldn't be happy with Guy, & I have written to tell him so." Mrs. Rivers looked startled. "What has happened, my love?" she asked anxiously. "I hope you have not been quarrelling. Guy is a good boy." "No, we have not been quarrelling—at least, not exactly. But I have thought it all over. Guy & I would never get on. And I am going to accept Lord Breton!" "Good gracious, my dear!" cried Mrs. Rivers, in mingled horror & admiration at her daughter's sudden decision. "But what will Guy say? . . . Have you reflected? . . ." "I have set Guy free; therefore I am at liberty to accept Lord Breton." "But—so soon? I don't understand," said poor Mrs. Rivers, in humble perplexity. "Of course the engagement will not be announced at once; but Lord Breton's letter requires an answer & I have written it." She handed the note to her mother, who looked over it with her usual doubtful frown, but whose only comment was a meek suggestion that it was very short. "I can't write four pages to say I'll accept him," said Georgie, sharply; & Mrs. Rivers, reflecting that her unusual crossness was probably due to concealed agitation, only said mildly, "but poor Guy." "Why do you pity Guy, Mamma? He will be rid of me, & if he *is* really in love with me—why, men get over those things very quickly." "But I cannot help thinking, my dear . . ." "Don't, Mamma!" cried Georgie, passionately, "don't think. I have made up my mind, & if you talk all day you can only make me cry." The last word was almost a sob, & Georgie turned sharply away from her mother. "I am afraid you are unhappy, darling child." "Why should I be?" burst out Georgie, with sudden fierceness. "Don't be so foolish Mamma! Why should I be unhappy? It is my own choice, & I don't want to be pitied!" She ran out of the room as she ended, & Mrs. Rivers' anxious ears heard her bedroom door slam a moment later. The note was sent duly, that morning; & in the afternoon the various members of the family saw, from their respective windows, Lord Breton of Lowood ride up to the door of Holly Lodge. Georgie, with an unusual colour in her face, which was set off by the drooping ruffle of lace about her soft throat, came in to her mother's room for a kiss & a word or two. Now that Guy's ring had really been sent back, she seemed to have nerved herself to go through the day resolutely; & with a quick, firm step, & her head higher than its wont she went downstairs to meet her suitor. Lord Breton was leaning against the mantel-piece where Guy had stood yesterday; & it would have been hard to find a greater contrast to that handsome young gentleman than Georgie's noble lover. Fifty-eight years of what is commonly called hard living had left heavy traces

13

on what in its day was known as a fine figure; & in the Lord
Breton whom some few could remember as "that gay young
buck" the present generation saw nothing but a gray gouty
old gentleman, who evidently enjoyed his port wine & sherry
generously. He came forward as Georgie entered, & bending
over her hand (it was not the hand that Guy had kissed) said,
pompously: "I need not say how deeply I feel the honour you
confer on me, Miss Rivers. This is indeed a happy day!"
"Thank you," said Georgie, with a wild desire to draw her
hand away; "you are very kind, Lord Breton." "No, no," returned his lordship affably; "I only rejoice in being allowed to
call mine a young lady so abundantly endowed with every
charm as Miss Rivers—as—May I call you Georgina?" Georgie
started; no one had ever called her by her name, preferring the
boyish abbreviation which seemed to suit her lively, plump
prettiness best; but, after all, it was better he should not call
her as Guy did. Georgina was more suitable for the future Lady
Breton. "You have won the right to do so," she said, as she sat
down, & Lord Breton took a chair opposite, at an admiring
distance. "A most precious right," he replied, conjuring up the
ghost of what some might recall as a fascinating smile; but
which was more like a bland leer to the eye unassisted by
memory. "Let me assure you," he continued, "that I know how
little a man of my advanced years deserves to claim the attention of a young lady in the lovely bloom of youth; but—ahem—
I hope that the name, the title—& above all the respect &
esteem which I lay at her feet may compensate—" he paused,
& evidently wondered that Georgie did not reply to this sublime condescension; but as she was silent, he was forced to take
up the thread of his speech. "As I said in my letter, you will

remember, Miss . . . Ah . . . Georgina—as I said in my letter,
I do not see why difference of age should be an obstacle to a
happy union; & as—ahem—& since your views so happily coin-
cide with mine, permit me to—to adorn this lovely hand with
—a—with—" here Lord Breton, finding that his eloquence had
for the moment run dry, supplied the lack of speech by action,
& producing a brilliant ruby set in large diamonds, slipped it
on Georgie's passive hand. "I hope you will accept this, as a
slight token of—of . . ." "It is very beautiful," said Georgie,
colouring with pleasure, as the dark fire of the ruby set off the
whiteness of her hand. "You are most generous. But you will
forgive me if I do not wear it, at least in public. I should prefer
not to have the engagement announced at once." Lord Breton
looked vastly astonished, as he might have done if a crossing-
sweeper to whom he had tossed a shilling had flung it back in
his face. "May I ask why this—this secrecy must be preserved?"
he said, in a tone of profound, but suppressed, indignation; remembering, just in time, that though the wife is a legitimate
object of wrath, it is wise to restrain one's self during courtship. "I am going to shew you what a spoiled child I am, by
refusing to tell you," said Georgie, putting on an air of im-
perious mischievousness to hide her growing agitation, "& I
know you will humour me. I am so used to having my own
way, that it might be dangerous to deprive me of it!" If she
had not said this with a most enchanting smile, naughty & yet
appealing, Lord Breton might not have been so easily ap-
peased; but being charmed with this pretty display of wilfulness (as men are apt to be before marriage) & concluding that
her mother might have something to do with the obstruction
she would not name, he only said, with a bow, "The loss is on

my side, however! I shall count the days until I can proclaim to the world what a prize I have won." Georgie laughed; a sweet, little bird-like laugh, which was as resistless as her pout. "You pay me so many compliments that I shall be more spoiled than ever! But you will not have to wait long, I promise you." "No waiting can be very long while I am privileged to enjoy your companionship," said Lord Breton, rising to the moment triumphantly. "Oh, for shame! Worse & worse!" cried Georgie. "But I think Mamma is in the study. Won't you come in & see her?"

Chap. III. Jilted.

———— "There can be no reason
Why, when quietly munching your dry-toast & butter
Your nerves should be suddenly thrown in a flutter
At the sight of a neat little letter addressed
In a woman's handwriting." *Robert Lytton*: Lucile.

GUY HASTINGS WAS FINISHING an unusually late breakfast
at his favourite resort in London, Swift's Club, St. James St.,
on the morning after his parting with Georgie, when a note
addressed in her well-known hand, with its girlish affectation
of masculiness, was handed to him by a Club servant. Although he was surprised that she should have written so soon,
(she seldom, during his trips to London, wrote to him at all)
he was not excited by any stronger emotion than surprise &
slight curiosity, for the words that passed between them the
day before had appeared to him nothing more than a lover's
quarrel developed by bad weather & ennui & he was too well
accustomed to unaccountable phases in his cousin's April character to imagine that anything serious could be its consequence.
A man, however, who is as deeply in love as Guy was, does not
have a letter in the beloved one's handwriting long unopened;
& though a pile of other envelopes "To Guy Hastings Esqr."
were pushed aside until fuller leisure after breakfast, he broke
Georgie's seal at once. One glance at the hurriedly written

lines sufficed to change the aspect of life completely. At first
there came a sense of blank bewilderment, followed, upon reflection, by indignation at this undeserved slight; & these emotions combined were enough to make him turn from the break-
fast-table, thrusting the package which contained the ring into
his breast-pocket, to escape from the clatter & movement of the
breakfast room. One might have supposed that every member
of the club would be off shooting, fishing, hunting or travelling at this unfashionable time, but of course, as Guy went
down to take refuge in the reading-room he was fastened upon
by a veteran club bore, who talked to him for half an hour by
the clock, while all the time Georgie's note was burning in his
pocket. At last the bore discovered that he had an engagement, & with deep regret (more for Guy's sake than his own)
was obliged to break off in the midst of an Indian anecdote;
but he was replaced almost immediately by Capt. Doublequick of the ____th, who always had a new scandal to feast
his friends on, & now for dearth of listeners, came to tell Guy
the fullest details of "that affair with young Wiggins & the
little French Marquise." This delectable history, embellished
with the Capt.'s usual art, lasted fully another half hour; &
Guy was in the last stages of slow torture when the unconscious Doublequick espied a solitary man at the other end of
the room who had *not* heard all about "young Wiggins." Left
to himself, Guy, with the masculine instinct of being always
as comfortable as possible, settled himself in an armchair, &
reread Georgie's note, slowly, carefully & repeatedly, as
though he fancied it might be an optical delusion after all.
But it was one of Georgie's virtues to write a clear hand. The
cruel words were there, & remained the same, read them as he

would. At last, as he sat half-stupidly staring at the few lines, a purpose formed itself within him to write at once & ask the meaning of them. Think as he would, he could not remember having, by word or act, justified Georgie in sending him such a letter; & he concluded that the best thing & the simplest he could do, was to demand an explanation. He loved her too deeply & reverently to believe that she could mean to throw him over thus; he thought he knew the depths & shallows of her character, & though he was not blind to her faults, he would never have accused her, even in the thought, of such unwarranted heartlessness. Having determined, then, on this first step, he called for pen & paper, & after tearing up several half-written sheets, folded & sealed this letter.

What have I done to deserve the note I got from you this morning? Why do you send the ring back? God knows I love you better than anyone on earth, & if I am at fault, it is ignorantly. If you have found out you don't care for me, tell me so—but for Heaven's sake don't throw me over in this way without a word of explanation. G.H.
Miss Rivers. Holly Lodge, Morley-near-W. Adamsbro.

Every one of those few words came straight from Guy's heart; for Georgie Rivers had been his one "grande passion," & his love for her perhaps the noblest, strongest feeling he was capable of. Indeed, I am disposed to think that the life of "a man about town" (the life which Guy had led since his college days five years before) is apt to blunt every kind of feeling into a well-bred monotone of ennui, & it is a wonder to me that he had preserved so strong & intact the capacity of really "falling in love." Of course, he had had a dozen little affaires de coeurs here & there before his heart was really touched; a man who lives as fast & free as Guy Hastings had done, seldom escapes without "the least little touch of the spleen"—but he had outgrown them one after another as people do outgrow those inevitable diseases, until the fatal malady seized him in the shape of his pretty cousin. His love for her had influenced his whole life, & blent itself into his one real talent, for painting, so that he sketched her bewitching little head a thousand & one times, & looked forward in the future, after his marriage, to turning his brush to account, selling his pictures high, &, in the still dimmer To-be becoming an R.A. How many an idle amateur has dreamed in this fashion! Meanwhile, he had enjoyed himself, made love to her, & lived neither better nor worse than a hundred other young men of that large class delightful for acquaintance, but dangerous for matrimony, whom susceptible young ladies call "fascinating" & anxious mothers "fast." Now, though like takes to like, it is seldom that two people of the same social tastes fall in love with each other; Mr. Rapid, who has been in all the escapades going, & connected with a good many of the most popular scandals, is attracted by Miss Slow, just out of a religious boarding-school, with downcast eyes & monosyllabic conversation; Miss Rapid, who has always been what Punch calls "a leetle fast," settles down to domesticity with good, meek-minded Mr. Slow. Such is the time-honoured law of contrasts. But Guy Hastings & Georgie were one of those rare exceptions said to prove the rule which they defy. If Guy had tasted the good things of life generously, his cousin was certainly not wanting in a spice of fastness. Yet these two sinners fell mutually in love at first sight, & remained in that ecstatic condition until Georgie's unaccountable note seemed to turn the world temporarily up-side-down. That unaccountable note! After answering it & calling for a servant to post his answer, he thrust it away in his pocket, & since "there was no help for it," resolved to make the best of the matter by forgetting it as quickly as possible. There are few young men who do not turn with an instinct of abhorrence from the contemplation of anything painful; & some possess the art of "drowning dull care" completely. Guy, however, could not shake his disagreeable companion off; & he must have shewed it in his face, for as he was leaving the club, in the forlorn hope of finding some note or message from Georgie at his rooms, a familiar voice called out "Hullo, Guy Fawkes, my boy! I didn't know you were in town! Had a row? What makes your mustachios look so horridly dejected?" "Jack Egerton!" exclaimed Guy, turning to face the speaker, a short, wiry-built little man with reddish whiskers & honest gray eyes, who laid a hand on his shoulder, & gravely scanned him at arm's length. Guy laughed rather uneasily. No man likes to think that another has guessed his inmost feelings at first sight. "Yes," said Egerton, slowly, "your Fortunatus purse has run out again, & Poole has too much sense to send that blue frock coat home, or you've had a row about some pretty little votary of the drama, & been O jolly thrashed—or— Araminta, or Chloe or Belinda (we won't say which) has been shewing you some charming phase in her character usually reserved for post-nuptial display. Come now, Knight of the Dolorous Visage, which is it?" Jack Egerton (commonly called Jack-All, from his wonderful capacity for doing every-thing, knowing everybody & being everywhere) although by some years Guy's senior, had known him at Cambridge (poor

Jack was there through several sets of new men) & had struck up a warm friendship with him which nothing since had shaken. Egerton shared Guy's artistic inclinations, & was like him "a man about town," & a general favourite, so that the similarity of their life had thrown them together ever since they forsook the shade of Alma Mater, Jack steering the "young Duke" as he always called Guy, out of many a scrape, & Guy replenishing Jack's purse when his own would allow of such liberality. Guy then, who would not have betrayed himself to any other living man, found it a great relief to unburden his woes to Jack Egerton, knowing that he possessed the rare talent of keeping other people's secrets as jealously as his own. "Hang it, there *is* a row," said the lover, pulling the dejected moustache. "But for Heaven's sake come out of this place. We shall be seized upon by some proses in a minute. Come along." He ran his arm through Egerton's, & the two sallied forth into the streets, making for the deserted region of Belgravia. It was not until they were in the most silent part of that dreary Sahara between the iron railings of a Duke who was off in Scotland, & the shut windows of an Earl who had gone to Italy, that Jack, who knew his companion "au fond," broke the silence by, "Well, my boy?" Guy glared suspiciously at a dirty rag-picker who was expressing to himself & his rag-bag the deepest astonishment "that them two young swells should be 'ere at this time o' year"; but even that innocent offender soon passed by, & left him secure to make his confession in entire privacy. "Look here" he said, taking Georgie's note from his pocket & handing it to Egerton. (Although the engagement between them, which had been of short duration, was kept private, he was shrewd enough to guess that his friend knew of it.) Jack, leaning against the Duke's railings, perused the short letter slowly; then folded it up & relieved himself by a low whistle. "Well?" groaned Guy, striking his stick sharply against His grace's area-gate, "What do you think of that? Of course you know that we were engaged, & she always said she cared for me, & all that—until *that* thing came this morning." Jack looked meditatively at his friend. "I beg pardon," he said, slowly, "but did you have a row when you last saw her?" "No, upon my honour none that I was conscious of! It was yesterday —beastly weather, you remember, & we were a little cross, but we made it up all right—at least, I thought so." "Of course you thought so," said Jack, calmly; "The question is, who provoked the quarrel?" "God knows—if there was a quarrel—I did not. I would go to the ends of the earth for her, Jack!" "Then— excuse me again, old boy—then *she* tried to pick a quarrel?" Guy paused—it seemed treason to breathe a word against his lady, & yet he could not but recall how strange her behaviour had been—"I—I believe I bored her," he stammered, not caring to meet Jack's eyes. "Did she tell you so?" "Well—yes; but, you know, she often chaffs, & I thought—I thought . . ." "You thought it was a little love-quarrel to kill time, eh?" said Jack, in his short, penetrating way. "Well, my dear boy, so it might have been, but I don't think it was." "What do you think then?" said Guy, anxiously. "Don't be afraid to tell me, old fellow." "Look here, then. You are a handsome young gaillard —just the sort that women like, the worse luck for you!—& I haven't a doubt your cousin (she shall not be named) fell in love with you. But—taking a slight liberty with the proverb— "fall in love in haste, repent at leisure"—How much have you got to support a wife on?" "Deucedly little," said Guy, bitterly. "Exactly. And you like to live like a swell, & have plenty of money to pitch in the gutter, when society requires it of you. Now, I dare say your cousin knows this." "Well?" "Well—& she has more good sense & just as much heart as most young ladies of our advanced civilization. She has had the wit to see what you, poor fool, sublimely overlooked—that what is comfort for one is pinching for two (or—ahem! three)—& the greater wit to tell you so before it is too late." Jack paused, & looked Guy directly in the face. "Do you understand?" "I don't know . . . I . . . for Heaven's sake, Jack, out with it," groaned the lover. Jack's look was of such deep, kindly pity as we cast on a child, whom we are going to tell that its goldfish is dead or its favourite toy broken. "My poor boy," he said, gently, "don't you see that you have been—jilted?"—

Chap. IV. The End of the Idyl.

> "Through you, whom once I loved so well—
> Through you my life will be accursed."

GEORGIE HAD JUST COME home from a ride to the meet with Lord Breton, on the day after her engagement to that venerable peer, when her mother called to her that there was a letter on her table upstairs in Guy's handwriting. Georgie changed colour; she had not expected this, & had thought to cast off "the old love" more easily. It came now like a ghost that steals between the feaster & his wine-cup; a ghost of old wrongs that he thought to have laid long ago but that rises again & again to cast a shadow on life's enjoyments. Georgie, however, determined to take the bull by the horns, & went up to her room at once; but she paused a moment before the pier-glass to smile back at the reflection of her trim figure in the dark folds of a faultless habit, & crowned by the most captivating little "topper" from under which a few little brown curls *would* escape, despite the precaution which Georgie of course *always* took to brush them back into their place. Then, setting her saucy, rose-bud mouth firmly, she turned from the glass & opened Guy's letter. If she had not been very angry at his having written at all, she might have been in danger of giving Lord Breton the slip, & coming back to her first choice; for she did love Guy, though such a poor, self-despising thing as love could have no legitimate place in the breast of the worldly-wise Miss Rivers! But she *was* angry with Guy, & having read his appeal tore it up, stamped her foot & nearly broke her riding-whip in the outburst of her rage. After that, she locked her door, & threw herself into what she called her "Crying-chair"; a comfortable, cushioned seat which had been the confidante of many a girlish fit of grief & passion. Having cried her eyes into the proper shade of pinkness, all the while complaining bitterly of Guy's cruelty & the hardness of the world, & her own unhappy fate, she began to think that his letter must nevertheless be answered, & having bathed her injured lids and taken an encouraging look at Lord Breton's ruby flashing on her left hand, she wrote thus:

My dear Guy: I don't think I deserved your reproaches, or, if I did, you must see that I am not worth your love. But I will tell you everything plainly. Knowing (as I said before) that we could never be happy together, I have engaged myself to Lord Breton. You will thank me some day for finding our feelings out & releasing you before it was too late—though of course I expect you to be angry with me now. Believe me, I wish that we may always be friends; & it is for that reason that I speak to you so frankly. My engagement to Lord Breton will not be announced yet. With many wishes for your happiness, Yours

"Georgina" Rivers.
To Guy Hastings Esqr. Swift's Club, Regent St. London W.

Georgie was clever & politic enough to know that such desperate measures were the only ones which could put an end to this unpleasant matter; but she was really sorry for Guy

& wanted to make the note as kind & gentle as possible. Perhaps Guy felt the sting none the less that it was so adroitly sheathed in protestations of affection & unworthiness. He was alone in the motley apartment, half-studio, half smoking-room & study, which opened off his bedroom at his London lodgings. He had not had the heart to stay at the Club after he had breakfasted; but pocketed Georgie's note (which was brought to him there) & went home at once. Inevitable business had detained him in town the day before, but he had determined to run down to West Adamsborough that morning, having prepared Georgie by his note. Now his plans, & indeed his whole life, seemed utterly changed. There comes a time in the experience of most men when their faith in womankind is shaken pretty nearly to its foundations; & that time came to Guy Hastings as he sat by his fire, with a bust of Pallas (adorned by a Greek cap & a faded blue breast-knot) presiding over him, & read his dismissal. But here I propose to spare my reader. I suppose every lover raves in the same rhetoric, when his mistress plays him false, & when to you, Sylvia, or you, Damon, that bitter day comes, you will know pretty accurately how Guy felt & what Guy said. Let us, then, pass over an hour, & reenter our hero's domain with Jack Egerton, who, at about 11 o'clock, gave his sharp, short rap at the door of that sanctum. "Who the devil is it?" said Guy, savagely, starting at the sound. "Your Mentor." "Jack?—Confound you!—Well, come in if you like." "I do like, most decidedly," said Egerton briskly, sending a puff of balmy Havana smoke before him as he entered. "What's the matter *now*? I've been at Swift's after you, & didn't half expect to find you moping here." "I don't care where I am," said Guy with a groan. "Sit down. What is the use of living?" "Shall I answer you from a scientific, theological or moral point of view?" "Neither. Don't be a fool." "Oh," with a slight shrug, "I thought you might like me to keep you company." Guy growled. "I don't know whether you want to be kicked or not," he said, glaring at poor Jack, "but I feel deucedly like trying it." "Do, my dear fellow! If it will shake you out of this agreeable fit of the dumps I shall feel that it is not paying too dearly." Guy was silent for a moment; then he picked up Georgie's letter & held it at arm's length, before his friend. "Look there," he said. Jack nodded. "My death warrant." He stooped down & pushed it deep into the smouldering coals—it burst into a clear flame, & then died out & turned to ashes. "Woman's love," observed Jack sententiously. Jack was a boasted misogynist, & if he had not pitied Guy from the depths of his honest heart, might have felt some lawful triumph in the stern way in which his favourite maxim, "Woman is false" was brought home to his long unbelieving friend; such a triumph as that classic bore, Mentor, doubtless experienced when Telemachus broke loose from the rosy toils of Calypso. "There," he continued. "If you have the pluck to take your fancy—your passion—whatever you choose to call it, & burn it as you burned that paper, I have some hopes for you." Guy sat staring absently at the red depths of the falling fire. "Did a woman ever serve you so, Jack?" he asked, suddenly, facing about & looking at Egerton sharply; but Jack did not flinch. "No," he said in a voice of the profoundest scorn; "I never gave one of them a chance to do it. You might as well say, did I ever pick up a rattle-snake, let it twist round my arm & say: 'Bite!' No, decidedly not!" "Then you believe that all women are the same?" "What else have I always preached to

you?" cried Jack, warming with his favourite subject. "What
does Pope say? 'Every woman is at heart a rake'! And Pope
knew 'em. And I know 'em. Look here; your cousin is not the
only woman you've had to do with. How did the others treat
you? Ah—I remember the innkeeper's daughter that vacation
in Wales, my boy!" "Don't," said Guy reddening angrily. "It
was my own fault. I was only a boy, & I was a fool to think
I cared for the girl—that's nothing. *She* is the only woman I
ever loved!" "So much the better. The more limited one's experience, the less harm it will do. Only guard yourself from
repeating such a favourite folly." "There's no danger of that!"
"I hope not," said Egerton. "But I have got a plan to propose
to you. After such a little complaint as you have been suffering
from, change of scene & climate is considered the best cure.
Come to Italy with me, old fellow!" "To Italy!" Guy repeated.
"When? How soon?" "The day after tomorrow." "But—I—I
meant—I hoped . . . to see her again." Jack rapped the floor
impatiently with his stick. "What? Expose yourself to the contempt & insult, or still worse, the pity, of a woman who has
jilted you? For Heaven's sake, lad, keep hold of your senses!"
"You think I oughtn't to go, then?" said Guy, anxiously. "Go!
—out of the fryingpan into the fire I should call it," stormed
Jack, pacing up & down the littered room. "No. He must be
a poor-spirited fellow who swims back for salvation to the
ship that his pitched him overboard! No. Come abroad with
me, as soon as you can get your traps together, & let the whole
thing go to the deuce as fast as it can." Jack paused to let his
words take effect; & Guy sat, with his head leaning on his
hand, still studying the ruins of the fire. At last he sprang up
& caught his shrewd-headed friend by the hand. "By Jove,

Jack, you're right. What have we got to live for but our art? Come along. Let's go to Italy—tomorrow, if you can, Jack!" And go they did, the next day. As his friends used to say of him, "Jack's the fellow for an emergency." His real, anxious affection for Guy, & his disinterested kind-heartedness conquered every obstacle to so hasty & unexpected a departure; & four days after he parted with Georgie in the drawingroom of Holly Lodge, Guy Hastings was on his way to Calais, looking forward, through the distorting spectacles of a disappointed love, to a long, dreary waste of life which was only one degree better than its alternative, the utter chaos of death.

Chap. V. Lady Breton of Lowood.

"A sorrow's crown of sorrow is remembering happier things."
Tennyson: Locksley Hall.

IT IS SOMETIMES WONDERFUL to me how little it takes to make people happy. How short a time is needed to bury a grief, how little is needed to cover it! What Salvandy once said in a political sense, "Nous dansons sur un volcan," is equally true of life. We trip lightly over new graves & gulfs of sorrow & separation; we piece & patch & draw together the torn woof of our happiness; yet sometimes our silent sorrows break through the slight barrier we have built to ward them off, & look us sternly in the face—

A month after Guy Hastings & Egerton started on their wanderings southward, Miss Rivers' engagement to Lord Breton of Lowood was made known to the fashionable world, & a month after that (during which the fashionable world had time to wag its tongue over the nine-day's wonder of the old peer's being caught by that "fast little chit") Georgie became Lady Breton. As a county paper observed: "The brilliant espousals were celebrated with all the magnificence of wealth directed by taste." Georgie, under her floating mist of lace went up the aisle with a slow step, & not a few noticed how intensely pale she was; but when she came out on her husband's arm her colour had revived & she walked quickly

& bouyantly. Of course Mrs. Rivers was in tears; & Kate &
Julia, in their new role of bridemaids fluttered about everywhere; & Miss Blackstone put on a gown of Bismarck-coloured
poplin (her favourite shade) & a bonnet of surprising form
& rainbow tints, in honour of the occasion. But perhaps the
real moment of Georgie's triumph was when the carriage
rolled through the grand gateways of Lowood, & after long
windings through stately trees & slopes of shaven lawn, passed
before the door of her new home. Her heart beat high as Lord
Breton, helping her to descend, led her on his arm through the
wide hall lined by servants; she felt now that no stakes would
have been too high to win this exquisite moment of possessorship. A fortnight after this brought on the bright, busy Christmas season; & as Lord Breton was desirous of keeping it
festively, invitations were sent out right & left. Georgie, although perhaps she had not as much liberty as she had
dreamed, found her husband sufficiently indulgent, unless his
express wishes were crossed; when, as the game-keeper once
remarked, "His lordship were quite *piq*nacious." She enjoyed,
too, the character of Lady Bountiful, & the tribute of ob-
sequious flattery which everybody is ready to pay to the mistress of a hospitable house; but it was not long before she felt
that these passing triumphs, which her girlish fancy had ex-
aggerated, palled on her in proportion as they became an
understood part of her life; praise loses half its sweetness when
it is expected. At first she would not confess to herself the
great want that seemed to be growing undefinably into her
life; but as the gulf widened, she could not overlook it. There
is but one Lethe for those who are haunted by a life's mistake;
& Georgie plunged into it. I have hinted that she had had a

reputation for fastness in her unmarried days; this reputation, which grew as much out of a natural vivacity & daring as out of anything marked in her conduct, grew to be a truth after she became Lady Breton. She dashed into the crowd to escape the ghosts that peopled her solitude with vague reproaches; & as the incompleteness of her mischosen life grew upon her day by day it gave new impetus to the sort of moral opium-eating which half-stifled memory. Lord Breton did not care to stay her; he took a certain pride in the glitter that his young wife's daring manners carried with them; for in pretty women, fastness has always more or less fascination. And Georgie had to perfection the talent of being "fast." She was never coarse, never loud, never disagreeably masculine; but there was a re-sistless, saucy élan about her that carried her a little beyond the average bounds laid for a lady's behaviour. It seemed as though her life never stood still, but rushed on with the hurry & brawl of the streamlet that cannot hide the stones clogging its flow. Altogether, she fancied herself happy; but there were moments when she might have said, with Miss Ingelow: "My old sorrow wakes & cries"; moments when all the hubbub of the present could not drown the low reproach of the past. It was a very thin partition that divided Georgie from her skeleton.

One day, when the last Christmas guests had departed from Lowood, & the new relay had not arrived, Lord Breton, who was shut up with a sharp attack of gout, sent a servant to Georgie's dressing-room, to say that he would like to see my lady. She came to him at once, for even his company, & his slow, pompous speeches, were better than that dreadful sol-itude; although gout did not sweeten his temper. "My dear," he said, "seeing that ivory chess-board in the drawing-room yesterday suggested to me an occupation while I am confined to my chair. I used to be a fair player once. Will you kindly have the board brought up?" As it happened, Georgie had not played a game of chess since the afternoon of her parting with Guy, & her husband's words, breaking upon a train of sad thought (she had been alone nearly all day) jarred her strangely. "Chess!" she said, with a start. "Oh, I—I had rather not. Excuse me. I hate chess. Couldn't we play something else?" Lord Breton looked surprised. "Is the game so repugnant to you that I may not ask you to gratify me this afternoon?" he asked, serenely; & Georgie felt almost ashamed of her weakness. "I beg your pardon," she said. "I play very badly, & could only bore you." "I think I can instruct you," said Lord Breton, benignly; mistaking her aversion for humility, & delighted at the display of this wife-like virtue. "Oh, no, indeed. I am so stupid about those things. And I don't like the game." "I hoped you might conquer your dislike for my sake. You forget that I lead a more monotonous existence than yours, when confined by this unfortunate malady." Lord Breton's very tone spoke unutterable things; but if Georgie could have mastered her feeling, the spirit of opposition alone would have been enough to prick her on now. "I am sorry," she said, coldly, "that my likes & dislikes are not under better control. I cannot play chess." "You cannot, or will not?" "Whichever you please," said Georgie, composedly. Lord Breton's wrath became evident in the contraction of his heavy brows; that a man with *his* positive ideas about wifely submission, & marital authority, should have his reproofs answered thus! "I do not think," he observed, "that you consider what you are saying." "I seldom do," said Georgia, with engaging frankness. "You know I am quite incorrigible." "I confess, Lady Breton, I do not care for such trifling." "I was afraid I was boring you. I am going to drive into Morley. Shall I order you any books from the library?" enquired Georgie, graciously. But as she rose to go, Lord Breton's ire burst out. "Stay!" he exclaimed, turning red up to his rough eye-brows. "I repeat, Lady Breton, that I do not think you know what you are saying. This trivial evasion of so simple [a] request displeases me; & I must again ask you to sacrifice part of your afternoon to the claims of your husband." Georgie, who [was] standing with her hand on the door, did not speak; but her eyes gave him back flash for flash. "Will you oblige me by ringing for the chess-board?" continued Lord Breton, rigidly. "Certainly. Perhaps you can get Williamson to play with you," said Georgie, pulling the bell. (Williamson was my lord's confidential valet.) "I beg your pardon. I believe I have already asked *you* to perform that function, Lady Breton." "And I believe that I have already refused," said Georgie, retaining her coolness in proportion as her husband grew more irate. At this moment, Williamson appeared, & Lord Breton ordered him to bring up the chess-board. When he was gone, Georgie saw that matters had gone too far for trifling. She had set her whole, strong will against playing the game, & she resolved that Lord Breton should know it at once. "I do not suppose," she said, looking him directly in the face, "that you mean to drive me into obeying by force. Once for all, I cannot & I will not, do as you ask me. You have insulted me by speaking to me as if I were a perverse child, & not the head of your house; but I don't mean to lose my temper. I know that gout is very trying." With this Par-

thian shot, she turned & left the room. Lord Breton, boiling
with rage, called after her—but what can a man tied to his
chair with the gout do against a quick-witted strategist in pet-
ticoats? Lord Breton began to think that this wife-training was,
after all, not mere child's play. This was the first declaration
of open war; but it put Lord Breton on the alert, & spurred
Georgie into continual opposition. After all, she said to herself, quarrelling was better than [the] heavy monotony of
peace; Lord Breton was perhaps not quite such a bore when
worked into a genuine passion, as when trying to be ponderously gallant. Poor Georgie! When she appeared on her husband's arm at the county balls & dinners in the flash of her
diamonds & the rustle of her velvet & lace, it seemed a grand
thing to be Lady Breton of Lowood; but often, after those very
balls & dinners, when she had sent her hundred-eyed maid
away, & stood before the mirror taking off her jewels, she felt
that, like Cinderella, after one of those brief triumphs, she was
going back to the ashes & rags of reality.

Chap. VI.   At Rome.

"I & he, Brothers in art." *Tennyson.*

A LARGE STUDIO on the third floor of a Roman palazzo; a
room littered & crowded & picturesque in its disorderliness, as
only a studio can be. A white cast of Aphrodite relieved by a
dull tapestry background representing a wan Susannah dip-
ping her foot in the water, while two muddy-coloured elders
glare through a time-eaten bough; an Italian stove surmounted
by a coloured sporting print, a Toledo blade & a smashed
Tyrolean hat; in one corner a lay-figure with the costumes of
a nun, a brigand, a sultana & a Greek girl piled on indiscriminately; in another an easel holding a large canvas on
which was roughly sketched the head of a handsome contadina.
Such was the first mixed impression which the odd furnishing
of the room gave to a newcomer; although a thousand lesser
oddities, hung up, artist-fashion, everywhere, made a background of bright colours for these larger objects. It was a soft
February day, & the window by which Guy Hastings sat (he
was lounging on its broad, uncushioned sill) was opened; so
that the draught blew the puffs from his cigarette hither &
thither before his face. Jack Egerton, who shared the studio
with him, was painting before a small easel, adding the last
crimson touches to a wild Campagna sunset, & of course they
kept the ball flying between them pretty steadily, as the one

worked & the other watched. "That will be a success," observed Guy, critically. "For whom did you say it was painted?" "A fellow named Graham, an English merchant, with about as much knowledge of art as you & I have of roadmaking. But it is such a delightful rarity to sell a picture, that I don't care who gets it." "How did he happen to be trapped?" Jack laughed. "Why, I met him at your handsome Marchese's the other day, & she made a little speech about my superhuman genius, which led him to take some gracious notice of me. I hinted that he might have seen one of my pictures (that confounded thing that Vianelli's had for a month) in a shop-window on the Corso, & he remembered it, & enquired the price. 'Very sorry' said I, 'but the thing is sold. To an English Earl, an amateur, whose name I am not at liberty to mention.' He gobbled the bait at once, ordered this at a splendid price, & I ran down to Vianelli's, let him into my little game, told him to send the picture home at once, & then sent some flowers to the Marchese!" Guy laughed heartily at his friend's ruse, & then observed, "I wish you had mentioned that *I* had some pictures which I would part with as a favour." "By degrees, my boy, by degrees. He will come to the studio, to see this chef-d'oeuvre, & then you shall be introduced as a painter of whose fame he has of course etc., etc. By the way, I shouldn't wonder if he came today." Guy knocked the ashes off his cigarette & got up from his seat. "I thought Teresina would have come this morning," he said, "but I hope she won't. She gets so confoundedly frightened when anybody comes in, & one feels like such a fool." "Guy!" said Egerton, suddenly, laying down his brush. "Well, old fellow?" "Are you going to make an ass of yourself?" "Not that I know of. How do you mean?" Guy stood opposite his friend, & looked him frankly in the face. "I mean," said Jack, resuming his work, "Are you going to fancy yourself in love with this pretty little peasant, & get into no end of a scrape?" "I don't know." "Well, then, be warned. What is the saying? Le jeu ne vaut pas la chandelle." "Very likely not. But . . . Ah, here she is. I know that tremulous little knock." Guy opened the door as he spoke, to admit a contadina, in holyday dress, with a gold chain about her soft olive throat & a clean white head-dress above her lustrous braids pinned with a silver dagger. She could not have been more than 16 years old, & was of that purest type of the Roman peasant which is so seldom met with nowadays. Her large, languid blue-black eyes were so heavily fringed that when she looked downward (as she almost always did, from an instinct of fawn-like timidity) they scarcely gleamed through their veil; & there was not a tinge of colour in the transparent olive cheek which made her full, sensitive mouth look all the redder as it parted on a row of pearl-white teeth, when Guy greeted her with his usual gentle gayety. It was no wonder that Jack had his fears. Little Teresina, with her trembling shyness & her faint smiles, & her low, sweet Italian, was a more dangerous siren than many an accomplished woman of the world. "I expected you" said Guy, smiling, as she stepped timidly into the room; & speaking in Italian, which Jack, as he bent quietly over his work, wished more than ever to understand. "Look here," Guy continued, pointing to the sketched head in the corner, "I have not touched it since because I knew I could not catch those eyes or that sweet, frightened smile without looking at you again." As he spoke, he moved the easel out into its place, & began to collect his brushes, while Teresina went quietly to place herself in a large, carved armchair raised on a narrow daïs. When Guy had finished his preparations, & arranged the light to his complete satisfaction, he sprang up on the daïs, with an old red cloth on his arm & stretched it at Teresina's feet. "Now, piccola," he said, standing at a critical distance, "let us see if you are properly posed. Wait a minute. So." He came close to her, adjusted a fold in her dress & moved her soft, frightened hand a little. "Are you so much afraid of me, cara?" he asked, smiling, as he felt it tremble. "I am not very hard to please, am I?" Teresina shook her head. "There," said Guy, "that is right, now. Only lift up those wonderful lashes. I do not want to paint the picture of a blind contadina, do I?" All this, spoken in a soft tone which was natural to Guy when addressing any woman, made poor Jack groan inwardly at his own stupidity in not understanding that sweet pernicious language that sounded like perpetual love-making! Having perfected Teresina's attitude, Guy sat down before his canvas, & began to paint; every now & then saying something to provoke the soft, monosyllables that he liked so well. "Where did you get that fine gold necklace, piccola?" he asked, beginning to paint it in with a few preparatory touches. "It is not mine. It belongs to la madre," said Teresina. "She wore it at her wedding." "Ah, & perhaps you will wear it at yours. Should you like to get married, Teresina?" "I don't know," said Teresina, slowly. "La madre wants me to marry Pietro (the carpenter, you know) but I would rather kill myself!" There was a flash in the soft velvet eyes, that made Guy pause in undisguised admiration; but it died in an instant, & no art of his brush or palette could hope to reflect it. "Is there anyone else you would like to marry, Teresina?" She was silent; & he repeated his question. "Why do you ask me, Signore?" said the girl, dropping her lids. "I wish you would go on painting." Guy was not a little astonished at this outburst; & went on with his work quietly, to Jack's intense relief. After about an hour of silence (Jack was obstinately dumb during Teresina's presence in the studio, believing that those infernal models could understand anything a fellow said) a round knock at the door made Guy breathe a low "confound it!" Egerton called "Come in," & the next moment a portly gentleman, unmistakably English from top to toe, stood on the threshold. "Mr. Graham!" said Jack, rising. "You find me at work on the last touches of your little thing. Let me present my friend, Mr. Hastings, whose fame of course . . . I need not say. . . . Mr. Graham bowed, & was very much honoured by an introduction to Mr. Hastings. Mr. Graham spoke in a satisfied, important voice. Mr. Graham had the uneasy, patronizing air of a man who stands higher than his level, & is not quite sure of his footing. "You see," Jack continued, lightly, moving a chair forward for his august visitor, "that we painters are not quite such idle fellows as the world makes us out to be. Hastings & I take advantage of this fine light for our work." "So I observe," said Mr. Graham, with a bow. "I see you've nearly done my order—a very nice little bit (as you artists would say) a very nice little bit." As Mr. Graham spoke, his eye wandered about the motley room, & in its course rested on Teresina. As Guy had said, she got "so confoundedly frightened" when any stranger was present; it was the first year she had been hired as a model, & the miserable life had not yet rubbed off her girlish bloom. When she

41

met Mr. Graham's scrutinizing eyes, her lashes drooped & a soft crimson stole over her neck & face, making her lovelier than ever; "let me go, Signore," she whispered to Guy, who had approached her to rearrange some detail in her dress. Then, without a word, she slipped down from her elavation, & stole quickly out of the room, still followed by Mr. Graham's gaze. "A model, eh? A very pretty little girl, Mr. Hastings. And a very nice picture—a very good likeness." Mr. Graham threw his head back critically & fancied, worthy man, that he had been eminently calculated to discriminate justly in art. "Have you been long at that, eh?" he continued, nodding towards the picture. "Two sittings," said Guy, shortly; he was vexed that this intrusion had put his shy bird to the flight, & could not abide this goodnatured bourgeois patronage which Jack laughed at & professed to like as a study of character. "A very pretty, sweet little girl," said Mr. Graham, who had a weighty way of repeating his remarks as if they were too precious to pass at once into oblivion. "But I am told that those models haven't much character, Mr. Hastings, eh?" "A common mistake," Guy returned coldly. "Ah!" said Mr. Graham. But Jack's effusive politeness flattered him more than the stern reserve of Jack's handsome, sulky friend; & Guy was left to himself, while the merchant & Egerton talked together. It was not until the former rose to go, that he was again drawn into the circle of conversation. "I hope we shall see you at our apartment, no. 2 via _____, Mr. Egerton. You—Mr. Hastings— you also, Sir. I shall be happy to introduce my wife & daughter. I shall have my little commission tomorrow, then? Good morning to you, gentlemen." And Mr. Graham marched out with what (he flattered himself) was a ducal elegance of manner & carriage. When the door was shut, Guy relieved himself of, "I hate your confounded shopkeepers!" "Every man who buys my pictures is my brother," exclaimed Jack, dramatically, "whatever be his station in life!" "Odd—because I never knew one of your brothers to do such an ingenuous thing!" observed Guy, gathering up his brushes. "Guy, my boy! You're getting sarcastic." "Very likely. I am going to the deuce by grande vitesse." "Why don't you stop at a station by the way?" said Egerton, rising with a yawn from his easel. "It would be a pity to reach your destination so soon." "What does it matter?" returned Guy, bitterly, turning away to stare out of the window. "A good deal, my boy, to some people." "I might have thought so once," said Guy very low. Jack was silent; he lighted his cigar & leaned back in a medieval armchair puffing meditatively. After a while he said, "Are you falling in love with Teresina?" Guy started. "No," he said, "I don't think I am falling in love with anybody. If I have any heart left, I haven't enough for that. Poor little Teresina!" "Why do you pity her?" said Jack, sharply. "Because she is young &—I believe—sincere." "Pity such virtues don't last longer in persons of her class!" said Egerton." "But you've got her in your head. Now, what are you going to do with her?" "Paint her." "Nonsense!" Jack jumped up & laid a hand on his friend's shoulder. "Look here, my boy," he said, in his quick way, "since you left London with me last Autumn you have been doing your best to shew what I have always said—that there is nothing like a woman for ruining a man's life. In short, you have been going rapidly to the dogs. Well; I am not a parson either, & I don't care to preach. But, for Heaven's sake, don't give way one instant to another woman! If, as you say, this child is innocent & honest, leave her so. Don't let those confounded soft eyes twist you into the idea that you're in love." "Poor little Teresina!" said Guy again.

Chap. VII.   The Luckiest Man in London.

"Oh, to be in England, now that April's there."
Robert Browning: Dramatic Lyrics.

As the warm Roman Winter melted into Spring, Jack Egerton felt growing upon him the yearning which the poet expressed above; excepting that he would have transposed the month & made it May, or, in other words, "the season." In short, he got a little tired of his painting & the Bohemianism of his life in Rome; & would have been only too glad if he could have carried Guy off with him. But Guy would not go. His love had not been of the slight sort which can be cast off like a dress out of fashion, at the right time; & he dreaded being within reach of the possibility of seeing his cousin again. As it is with many another young man of like class & habits, the warp in his love had warped his life; an undertone of bitterness ran habitually through it now, which Jack had striven in vain to destroy. Guy had decided to spend the Summer in Alp-climbing; but he intended to stay on in Rome until the end of April, so that Jack, who started homeward in the early part of that month, left him still there. Jack got back to England in time to pay several duty visits to his relations in the country; but the opening season found him in London again, ready, as the phrase is, for everything "going." Everybody was glad to see "Jack-All" back again; but his welcome at Swift's was per-

haps the warmest & the most heartily gratifying that he got.
"Hullo, melancholy Jacques!" cried some familiar voice as
Jack stalked into the reading room one mild May evening.
"Back from Rome, eh? An R.A. yet?" More than one took up
the chorus; & Jack found himself surrounded by a group of
laughing flâneurs, all asking questions, "chaffing," & regaling
the newcomers with town news. "How's Hastings?" said a tall
Life-Guardsman (a Duke's son) who had joined in the circle
of talk over the broadcloth shoulder of a wiry little Viscount.
"Didn't Hastings go to Rome with you?" "Of course he did,"
said the Viscount, who knew everybody. "Don't you know,
Hasty was so awfully gone on old Breton's wife, & she jilted
him—didn't she, Jack? Stunning little woman!" "Yes," said
someone else, "Hasty was entirely done up by that. It *was* hard
lines." "Has Hasty gone in regularly for painting?" enquired
the Life Guard's man; & staunch Jack, who had not answered
a word to this volley, turned the subject dexterously. "Yes. He
has joined the Alpine Club." "Instead of the Royal Acad-
emy?" "Whoever made that witticism ought to be black-
balled," said the Viscount. "Can't you give Jack full swing, all
of you?" "By all means! Fire away, old boy. How many women
are you in love with, how many pictures have you sold & how
many people have you quarrelled with?" "I am in love with
as many women as I was before," said our stout misogynist, "&
I have sold two pictures" ("Why did you make him perjure
himself?" observed the Viscount parenthetically) "& I have
quarrelled with everybody who didn't buy the rest." There was
a general laugh; & just then Lord Breton (who was one of
the Patriarchs of the Club) came up & caught sight of Jack.
"Ha! Mr. Egerton. I understood you were in Italy," said his

lordship condescendingly. "Have you been long in town? If you have no prior engagement, dine with me tomorrow night at 8." And Lord Breton passed on with a bow, while Jack stood overwhelmed by this sudden condescension. "By Jove," said the Lifeguardsman as the old peer passed out of hearing, "I believe you're the luckiest man in London!" "Why?" said Jack, amused. "Why! Don't you know that you're going to dine with the fastest, handsomest, most bewitching woman in town? Don't you know that everybody's mad over Lady Breton?" "Yes!" added the Viscount. "Tom Fitzmore of the _____th & little Lochiel (Westmoreland's son, you know) had a row about her that might have ended seriously if the Duchess of Westmoreland hadn't found out & gone down on her knees to her eldest hope, imploring him to give it up. Lochiel is a muff, & went off to Scotland obediently, but Fitzmore was furious." "They say Monsieur is as watchful as a dragon & as jealous as an old woman, but she plays her cards too cleverly for him," resumed my lord Lifeguardsman. "I've danced with her once, & by Jove! it's like moving on air with a lot of roses & soft things in your arms." "And how she sings!" cried the Viscount, waxing warm. "I swear, it's a pity she's a lady. She'd make a perfect actress." "But old B. ('Beast' they call him you know—'Beauty & the Beast')," explained the other, "is awfully suspicious & never lets her sing except to a roomfull of dowagers & ugly men." "Thanks!" observed the quick-witted Viscount. "*I've* heard her sing twice." "Which proves the truth of my statement," quoth the Lifeguardsman coolly, lounging off towards another group, while the little nobleman, in a deep note of mock ferocity called after him for an explanation. This was not the last that Jack heard of

Lady Breton's praises. The next day he went to see a friend, a brother-artist (whose fame, however, exceeded Jack's) & saw on his easel the head of a woman with a quantity of white lace & pearls folded about a throat as round & soft as a Hebe's. Her soft, chesnut-brown hair fell in resistless little rings & wavelets about a low white arch of forehead, beneath which two brilliant hazel eyes, with curly fringes, glanced out with a half-defiant, half-enticing charm. The features, which had no especial regularity, were redeemed by the soft peachbloom on either rounded cheek, & the whole face made piquant by a small nose, slightly "tip-tilted," & a dimple in the little white chin. Although Jack could find no real beauty in the lines of the charmingly-poised head, some nameless fascination arrested his eyes; & he stood before the picture so long that the artist, who was just then busy with another portrait called out, "What! Are *you* losing your heart too, Benedick?" "Who is it?" said Jack. "What! don't you—It's the handsomest—no, not the handsomest, nor the most beautiful, nor the prettiest, woman in London; but, I should say, the most fascinating. Isn't that face irresistible? That is Lady Breton!" Jack started; perhaps he for the first time fully understood what had darkened Guy Hastings' life. "Yes," continued his friend, enthusiastically, "she is the sensation of the season. And no wonder! There is a perfect magic about her, which, I see by your face, I have been fortunate enough to reflect in part on my canvas. But if you knew her!" "I am going to dine there tonight," said Jack turning away, his admiration changed to a sort of loathing, as he thought of the destruction those handsome eyes had wrought. "Are you? Let me congratulate you. You're the luckiest man in London," cried the portrait-painter, uncon-

48

sciously repeating the words which had hailed Jack's good-
fortune at Swift's the night before. "And this," thought
Egerton, "is what a woman gets for spoiling a man's life!"
Nevertheless, prompted by a certain curiosity (which Jack was
careful to call a natural interest in the various phases of human
nature, since to confess the desire of seeing a woman—even the
woman whom all London was raving about—would have been
high-treason to his cherished misogynism)—actuated, I say, by
this feeling, he looked forward rather impatiently to the evening which was to introduce him to the famous Lady Breton; &,
as he was ushered by a resplendent Jeames up the velvet-spread
staircase of her Belgravian mansion, was aware of that pleasur-
able sensation with which an ardent play-goer awaits the lifting of the curtain upon the first scene of a new drama. How
the curtain lifted, what scenes it disclosed, & how unexpectedly
it fell, our next chapter will reveal.

Chap. VIII. Jack the Avenger.

"I have a heart tho' I have played it false." *Old Play.*

LADY BRETON WAS LEANING against the chimney-piece in her splendid drawing-room, hung with violet satin, & illuminated by sparkling chandeliers. Her black velvet dress set off the neatly-moulded lines of her figure, which seemed to have gained in height & stateliness since her unmarried days in Holly Lodge; & the low, square-cut bodice revealed a bosom the whiter by contrast to a collar of rubies clasped closely about the throat. She was watching, half-absently, the flash of her rings, as she leaned her chin upon one drooping hand; & was so absorbed in some silent reverie, that she scarcely noticed the pompous entrance of her lord & master, until that noble gentleman observed, "I have asked Egerton to dine here to-night. I believe you know him." "I?" said Georgie, starting slightly. "N—no—I do not know him." But she *did* know that he was Guy's friend & travelling companion. "A very gentlemanly fellow, & of good family," said Lord Breton, graciously, "though an artist." A moment later, &, fortunately for his peace of mind, just too late to catch these words, Mr. Egerton was announced. Lord Breton went ponderously through an introduction to "Lady Breton, my friend Mr. Egerton"; & then he found himself sitting in a very easy chair, with only a velvet-covered tea-table between himself & the most popular woman in London. Certainly, the charm of her face, her tone, her gesture, was irresistible. Her ease was so engaging, there was such a pretty spice of freedom in her speech & manner, her coquetry was so artless & original, that Jack had surely succumbed if he had not seen in this fascinating Lady Breton the destroyer of his friend's happiness. Ten minutes later, after another stray man, a distant relative of Lord Breton's, had made his appearance in dinner-array, Egerton had the whitest of hands lying on his coat-sleeve & was leading his hostess to the dining-room, in a very delightful frame of mind. The parti quarré was kept alive, during the elaborate courses of the dinner, by Lady Breton's vivacity; & as she employed herself in drawing Jack out (Jack was a clever talker) the two kept a constant flow of words circulating. Every moment, as he watched her & heard her voice, the fascination & the loathing increased together. In truth, Georgie had laid herself out to conquer this clever friend of Guy's; & she in part succeeded. When at last she rose, with her rich draperies falling about her & a deeper flush on her cheek, & swept out of the room, a dullness fell on the three men which Lord Breton's sublimity was not likely to relieve. Jack was glad when the time which etiquette orders to be devoted to nuts & wine (Lord Breton's wine was by no means contemptible) was over, & the gentlemen went to the drawing-room to join Georgie; nor was his pleasure impaired by the fact that Lord Breton soon challenged his other guest to a game of billiards. "Let us stay here, Mr. Egerton," said Georgie, with a smile. "It always makes my head ache to see Lord Breton play billiards. You don't mind staying?" Jack protested. "Ah! I see you are like all other men—you always flatter." "How can we help it when there is so much to flatter?" "That is a doubtful compliment, but I will take it at its best, as one must everything in this life. Do you take tea, Mr. Egerton?" Jack had an old-maid's passion for the fragrant brew, & watched with no small enjoyment the quick movements of Georgie's pretty hand as she filled & sweetened his cup. "There! You have got to pay for my services by getting up to fetch it, since you *will* plant yourself at the other end of the room," she said, laughing, as she handed it to him. "Thanks. I find that English tea is a different thing from Roman tea," said Jack, leaning back luxuriously, so that he could watch her as she sat opposite, in a charming négligeé attitude, as easy as his own. "But one doesn't go to Rome for tea! At least, I believe not," she said, taking up her cup. "What does one go to Rome for?" returned Jack; "as I sit here, in this charming drawing-room, with London on every side, I wonder how anyone can care to go abroad?" "Really," said Georgie, smiling, "your words have a double entendre. Is it my drawing-room, Mr. Egerton, or London that makes it hard to go abroad?" "To those who have the happiness of knowing you, I should say—both." "Unanswerable! Compliments always are —But do tell me, Mr. Egerton, if you have seen my cousin Guy—Mr. Hastings, lately?" She said it lightly, easily, in the tone she had used to rally & amuse him a moment before; there was no change in voice, or manner. Jack was disagreeably startled out of his train of lazy enjoyment; in the charm of her presence he had nearly forgotten his loyalty to Guy, but the lightness of her tone as she named him, brought all the horror jarringly back. He changed in a moment from the mere drawing room lounger, with a flattering repartee for every remark, into the stout friend & the "good hater." He was our old Jack Egerton again. For a moment he did not answer her; & as she appeared absorbed in the contemplation of the fan which she was opening & furling, perhaps she did not see the angry flash in his honest gray eyes. When he spoke she did look up, & with undisguised astonishment in her pretty face. "I think, Lady Breton," said Jack, sternly, "that you should be able to answer your own question." "What *can* you mean, Mr. Egerton? Why do you speak in that solemn oracular manner?" "Excuse me, Lady Breton," returned Jack; "I cannot speak in any other tone of my friend!" "Than the solemn & oracular?" said Georgie, mischievously. "You must pardon me," Egerton answered gravely," If I ask you not to speak so lightly on a subject which . . . which . . ." "Pray go on, Mr. Egerton," she said, in a low, taunting voice; & it urged him on, before he knew it, to utter the truth. "I believe," he returned quickly, "that we are speaking at cross-purposes, but since you give me permission I *will* go on & tell you frankly that I cannot sit still and listen to such mere trifling with his name from the woman who has ruined Guy Hastings' life." Her colour deepened, but her voice was quite controlled as she said, "I do not think I gave you permission to insult me." "Nor did I mean to insult you, Lady Breton; if I have, order me out of your drawing-room at once—but I must speak the truth." "Since when have you developped this virtue, Mr. Egerton? Well—" she set her lips slightly, "go on. I will listen to the truth." "You have heard what I said," Jack answered, coldly. "Let me see"—Jack noticed that she composed herself by an effort—"that I had ruined Guy—Mr. Hastings' life." "As you must ruin the life of any man who has the misfortune to love you. You know your power." "Well—suppose I do. Did you come from Rome to tell me this, Mr. Egerton?" she said, bitterly. "No. And I see that I shall repent having told you," said Jack. "Let us talk of something else." "Not at all! Since you broached the subject, it shall be your penalty to go on with it as long as I choose." "Are you so unused to the truth, Lady Breton, that even such harsh truths as these are acceptable?" "Perhaps." She paused, playing with her fan; then, suddenly, flashing one of her superb looks at him; "How you despise me!" she said. "You think I cared nothing for—for him?" "I cannot think that if you had cared for him, you would have thrown him over." "Ah—you know nothing of women!" "I believe" said Jack, very low, "I know too much of them." "And you despise them all, do you not?" she cried. "Yet—I have a heart." "My friend did not find it so," said Jack, pitilessly. Her eyes flashed; & she bit her lip (the blood had fled from her whole face) before she could answer. "How do you know that you are not wronging me?" "If I am wronging you, why is my friend's life cursed?" he exclaimed. "No, Lady Breton! The wrong is on your side, & when I think of him, & of what he might have been, I cannot help telling you so." Her agitation had increased perceptibly, & she rose here, as if to find a vent for it in the sudden movement. Jack could not help thinking how her pallour altered her. There ran through his head, half unconsciously, the wonderful words that describe Beatrix Esmond when she finds her guilt discovered: "The roses had shuddered out of her cheeks; she looked quite old." He waited for Georgie to speak. "What he might have been," she repeated slowly. "What have I done? What have I done?" "You have very nearly broken his heart." She gave a little cry, & put her hand against her breast. "Don't! Don't!" she said, wildly.

"I *did* love him, I *did* care—I believe my heart is nearly broken too!" She tried to steady her voice, & went on hurriedly. "I was young & silly & ambitious. I fancied I didn't care, but I did—did. I have suffered too, & the more bitterly because what you say is true. I *have* wronged him!" She sank down on a chair, hiding her face in her hands, & Jack, who had not expected this passionate outburst, was not a little appalled by what he had brought about. But it was too late now to undo it; Georgie was thoroughly shaken out [of] her habitual artificial composure. The mask had fallen off, & oh, how sadly, sadly human were the features behind it! "And you," she went on, "are the first who has dared to tell me what *I* have felt so long! I could almost thank you—" She paused once more, & Jack knew that her tears were falling, though she screened her face with one lifted hand. "Instead of that," he said, "you must forgive my frankness—my impertinence, rather—in speaking to you in this way." "No—no. I think I feel better for it," she almost whispered. "But one thing more. Does he—does he think of me as you do?" "Do not ask me," said Jack, gently. "I think of you with nothing but pity." "And he—he despises me? He thinks I do not care for him? Oh—it will break my heart. And yet," she went on, with a moan, "what else have I deserved? Oh, my folly, my folly! But *you* believe I do love him? You see how wretched, how—" She did not notice, that, as she spoke, leaning toward Jack with her hand half outstretched, Lord Breton's voice was sounding near the door; but Jack did. "Yes," he said, composedly, taking up an album, "these photographs are charming. Have you seen the last of the Princess of Wales?" Georgie's tact would ordinarily have exceeded his; but she had been carried far beyond external observances, &

55

could only sit silent, with white, compressed lips as the gentle-man entered. When Lord Breton came up to the tea-table, however, she rose, & said: "Will you excuse me? I do not feel quite well—it is very warm. Will you give me your arm?" She took her husband's arm & he led her to the door. "Lady Bret-on's delicate health is a continual source of anxiety to me," he explained as he came back. But circumstantial evidence was against Jack, & there was a scowl of suspicion beneath my lord's heavy politeness. A few days later, Egerton called at the house, but my lady was out; & although he saw her several times at balls & drums & races, always resplendent & always surrounded by a faithful retinue of adorers, he had no oppor-tunity of exchanging a word with her.

Chap. IX. Madeline Graham.

"The lady, in truth, was young, fair & gentle."
Robert Lytton: Lucile.

SINCE HIS PARTING with Georgie Rivers, & the disappointment of his love, Guy Hastings had been, as Jack expressed it: "going rapidly to the dogs." Now there are many modes of travelling on this road; the melodramatic one in which the dark-browed hero takes to murder, elopement, & sedition; the commonplace one in which drinking, gambling & duelling are prominent features; the precipitate one of suicide; & finally that one which Guy himself had chosen. He did not kill himself, as we have seen, nor did he run away with anyone, or fight a duel, or drink hard; but he seemed to grow careless of life, money & health, & to lose whatever faith & tenderness he had had in a sort of undefined skepticism. Perhaps this least perceptible is yet the most dangerous way of "going to the dogs"; it is like the noiseless dripping of lime-water which hardens the softest substance into stone. Guy's life was no longer sweet to him. He felt himself sliding away from all ties of kindliness & affection, & did not care to stay his course; he thought his heart was withered & that nothing could revive it. Perhaps the first thing that came near touching it, & shewed that it had any vitality left, was Teresina. Not that he loved her; Jack need not have been anxious on that score. But there is a dangerous sort of interest & pity which may too easily be mistaken for love, & which Guy felt towards the little contadina. She appealed to the heart he thought dead by her shyness & her soft, leaning temper; & to his eye by the rich, languid beauty which could in no way bring to his mind another kind of prettiness with which his bitterest memories were associated. He painted the girl over & over again, & interested himself in her; but whatever danger might have been in store was warded off by a confession that Teresina made one April morning, with blushes & tears, to the Signore. She was in love, poor little soul, with Matteo, old Giovanni the blacksmith's son; but Matteo was poor, & Teresina's parents had destined her to be the wife of the rich carpenter, Pietro. So she told Guy; & her story so completely enlisted his sympathy that he not only went to see the Padre & bribed him largely to let Teresina marry where her heart was, but wrote to Mr. Graham, who had bought one of his pictures, & got a nice little sum from the generous merchant. This was some time after Jack's departure, & a week after Guy left Rome for his Summer wanderings in Switzerland, followed by the gratitude of two honest peasant hearts.

The soft July day, a little more than two months after this, he was walking along the old covered bridge at Interlaken, when the sound of voices reached him from the other end, & a moment later a stout, fair lady, who seemed to move in an English atmosphere, so clear was her nationality, appeared with a girl by her side. The girl was tall & élancée, & bore an unmistakeable resemblance to the elder lady; & a few yards behind them Guy espied the florid, whiskered countenance of Mr. Graham. The merchant was the first to speak his recognition, in his usual loud tones, while the ladies fell back a little, & the girl began to sketch with her parasol. "Mr. Hastings here!" exclaimed Mr. Graham. "This is a surprise! Been here long, eh? Mrs. Graham, my dear, this is Mr. Hastings, the gentleman who painted that pretty little face you make so much of; this is my daughter, Mr. Hastings." These introductions over, Guy perforce turned his steps & recrossed the bridge with the family party. He talked to Mrs. Graham, while the girl walked behind with her father; but his quick artist's eye had taken in a glance the impression that she was thin, but well-built, & exquisitely blonde, with large blue eyes, almost infantine in their innocent sweetness. She spoke very little, & seemed retiring & unaffected; & he noticed that her voice was low & musical. As for Mrs. Graham, she may best be described as being one of a large class. She was comely & simple-mannered, intensely proud of her husband & her daughter, & satisfied with life altogether; one of those dear, commonplace souls, without wit or style, but with an abundance of motherliness that might cover a multitude of fashionable defects. Guy was universally polite to women, but Mrs. Graham's bland twaddle about hôtels, scenery & railway carriages (the British matron's usual fund of conversation when taking a relaxation from housekeeping on the continent) was not very absorbing, & his eyes wandered continually towards her daughter—Madeline, her father had called her. He wondered why the name suited her soft, blonde beauty so well; he wondered if she were as refined as she looked; & indulged in so many of those lazy speculations which a young man is apt to lavish on a beautiful girl, that Mrs. Graham's account of their journey over the Cornice was almost entirely lost to his inattentive ears. Finally, as they drew near home, Madeline stopped to fill

59

her hands with flowers, & he picked up her sunshade, falling back by her side to admire her nosegay. This young gentleman —who would have called himself "a man of the world" & thought he knew woman-kind pretty well, from the actress to the Duchess—had never seen before the phenomenon of an unsophisticated English beauty among the better classes. "I think that ladies' hands were made for gathering flowers," he observed. "It is the prettiest work they can do." Madeline blushed; "It is the pleasantest work, I think," she said, in her clear, shy tones, bending her tall head over her field-blossoms. Guy thought of "The Gardener's Daughter," & wondered whether her golden hair was as pale & soft as Madeline Graham's. "But you can paint them," the girl added. "How I envy you!" "If you are so fond of flowers, you should learn to paint them yourself, Miss Graham," said Guy. "Ah—if I could. I don't think I have any talent." "You must let me find that out," he returned, smiling. "I should like to teach you." Madeline blushed again; indeed, every passing emotion made her colour change & waver exquisitely. Guy liked to watch the wildrose flush deepen & fade on the pure cheek beside him; it was a study in itself to make an artist happy. "You know," he went on, "all talents are not developed at once, but lie dormant until some magic touch awakens them. Your love for flowers may help you to find out that you are an artist." "I am very fond of pictures," said Madeline, simply. "I love the Madonna heads with their soft, sweet eyes & blue hoods. But then, you know, I am no judge of art—Papa is." At another time, Guy would have smiled at this daughterly illusion; now it only struck him as a very rare & pretty thing. "One does not need to be a judge of art to love it," he said. "The discrimination comes later; but the love is inborn." She lifted her wide blue eyes shyly to his face. "I suppose you have both," she said, gravely. "Very little of either, I am afraid," said Guy, smiling. "I am little more than an amateur, you know." Just then, Mr. Graham, who had gone forward with his wife, called Madeline. "Come, come, my dear. It is getting damp & we must be off to our hotel. Our paths divide, here, eh? Mr. Hastings. Come & see us." "Goodbye," said Madeline, with a smile. "Goodbye," he answered; "shall you be at home tomorrow afternoon?" "Yes. I believe so. Shall we not, Mamma?" "What, my dear? Yes," nodded Mrs. Graham. "Do come, Mr. Hastings. It's a little dull for Madeline here." And they parted, Guy lifting his hat, & lingering a moment to watch them on their way. "A very nice young fellow, eh?" said Mr. Graham, as Madeline slipped her hand through his arm. "Excellent family. Excellent family." "And so polite," cried Mrs. Graham. "I declare he talked beautifully." "I think he is very handsome," said Madeline, softly. "And how clever he is, Papa." "Clever, eh? Yes—yes; a rising young fellow. And very good family." "But it's a wonder to me he took any notice of you, Maddy," observed Mrs. Graham. "Those handsome young men in the best society don't care for anything under an Earl's wife." "But he is a gentleman, Mamma!" said Madeline with a blush. The next afternoon, a servant was sent up to Mr. Graham's apartments at the Hôtel Belvidere with a card; which a maid carried into an inner room, where the following dialogue went on while the Hôtel servant waited. "Mr. Hastings, Mamma—what shall I do?" "See him, love. I am not suffering much." "Oh, Mamma, I can't leave you alone!" "With Priggett, my dear? Of course. Perhaps he might know of a physician." "Of course,

Mamma! I will see him. Ask the man to shew Mr. Hastings up." And when Guy was ushered into the stiffly-furnished sitting room a pale young lady with her crown of golden hair somewhat disturbed & her white dress rumpled, came forward to meet him. "Oh, Mr. Hastings . . ." "Has anything happened, Miss Graham?" The tears were hanging on Madeline's lashes & her quiet manner was changed for a trembling agitation. "Mamma has sprained her ankle," she said, "& Papa is away. He went to the Lauterbrunnen this morning, & an hour ago Mamma slipped on the staircase—" she ended rather abruptly by pressing her handkerchief to her eyes. "My dear Miss Graham, how unfortunate! Have you sent for a physician? Can I do anything for you?" "Oh, thanks," said Madeline, "we have got the maid & I have bound her ankle up, but we didn't know where to find a physician." "How lucky that I came!" Guy exclaimed. "I believe there is no good native doctor, but Sir Ashley Patchem is at my Hôtel & I will go back at once." "Oh, thank you, thank you!" Madeline could scarcely control her tears, as she held her hand out. "May I come back & see if I can help you in any other way?" Guy said, as he took it; & then he was gone, at a quick pace. Half an hour later, the famous London physician was in Mrs. Graham's room at the Hôtel Belvidere. "A very slight sprain, I assure you," he said, as Madeline followed him anxiously into the sitting-room. "Don't disturb yourself. Only have this sent for at once." He put a prescription in her hand, & as he left the room Guy came in again. "I am so much relieved," said Madeline, "& I don't know how to thank you." "What does Sir Ashley say?" "It is very slight, not at all dangerous. I am so thankful! But this prescription . . . I suppose one of the servants . . ." "Let me take it," said Guy. Then, glancing at his watch; "Mr. Graham ought to be here shortly, but you will send for me in case of need, Miss Graham? Are you sure that I can do nothing else?" "You have done so much," Madeline answered, with a smile. "No, I think everything is arranged, & as you say Papa will be here soon." "I will not delay the prescription, then. Goodbye, Miss Graham!" "Goodbye." She held out her hand again, as to a friend, & again he took it & pressed it for an instant. As he walked homeward in the soft Summer dusk, he had the pleasant feeling of a man who knows that he has gained the admiration & gratitude of a pretty, interesting girl by an easy service just at the right time. No man wins his way so easily as he who has the good luck to prove himself "a friend in need"; & Guy felt that in one day he had come nearer to Madeline Graham than months of casual acquaintance could have brought him.

Chap. X. At Interlaken.

"Through those days
Youth, love & hope walked smiling hand in hand."
Old Play.

IT IS CERTAIN that in this world the smallest wires work the largest machinery in a wonderful way. The twist that Mrs. Graham's foot took on the Hôtel staircase, led gradually up a ladder of greater events to a most unexpected climax, & influenced her daughter's life as the most carefully laid plans could perhaps not have done. Strangely & wonderfully, "Dieu dispose." The Grahams had not intended to remain over a week at Interlaken, & had all their Summer plans arranged after the approved tourist fashion. These plans Mrs. Graham's sprained ankle of course overset. Slight at the accident was, it tied her to her couch for five weeks at the least; & all that could be done was to accept the circumstances & engage the best rooms which the Hôtel Belvidere could offer, for that length of time. Mr. Graham was thoroughly disgusted. "To be mewed up in this hole," he complained to Hastings, "with nothing to do but look at the mountains out of one's bedroom windows. In fact, though the continent is very pleasant for a change & very nice to travel in, England's the place to be quiet in!" "Yes, I agree with you," said Guy; "but I hope this unfortunate accident won't frighten you off to England?" Mr.

Graham shook his head despondently! "I wish it could, my dear Hastings, I wish it could. But, you see, our Madeline is too delicate for the rough English weather, & as we've got to choose between Nice & Rome of course we'll go to Rome again." As for Madeline, she accepted the change with youthful adaptability, invented fancy-work for her mother, collected flowers, played on the rattling Hôtel piano which had been moved into her sitting-room, & took long walks with her father & Mr. Hastings. These walks, indeed, were the pleasantest part of her quiet, contented days; Mr. Hastings talked so well & got her such pretty wild-flowers, she said simply to her mother. And Mrs. Graham sighed. Madeline was a good, dutiful girl, & full of worship for her father; but perhaps she was not sorry when, on the morning which had been chosen for a long pilgrimage, Mr. Graham got some business letters which required immediate answers, & announced at the breakfast table that he could not go. "Oh, what a pity, John," said Mrs. Graham, from the sofa. "It is such a beautiful day, & Maddy has been counting on this walk." Madeline looked studiously at her plate, but the pink was beginning to flutter up into her cheek. "Nonsense!" said Mr. Graham. "Madeline shall go, of course. What do you suppose Hastings wants with an old fellow like me, eh? No, no, Mother; Madeline shall go & they will be only too glad to be rid of me." "Oh, Papa!" murmured Madeline. But when Guy Hastings appeared an hour later, she was ready in her gray walking dress, with a quantity of light blue veil floating about her leghorn hat & looped around her throat. There was a slight flush on her face, & she had never looked more lovely. "This morning was made for a walk," said Guy, as he stood by Mrs. Graham's couch. "But the one we

have planned is long. I hope we shall not tire Miss Graham."
"Oh, no," said Madeline, coming up, "but—Papa can't come
this morning." "Mr. Graham has some business letters to at-
tend to," explained Mrs. Graham. Guy glanced at Madeline;
"You are dressed," he said: "won't you trust to my guidance?"
Madeline stood still, blushing; but just then Mr. Graham came
in, & overhearing Guy's words, said warmly: "Yes, indeed she
will! Take good care of her, Hastings. I say, she will be glad
to have her old father out of the way." "Oh, Papa," said
Madeline again. So the two started out, Guy carrying her
flower-basket & shawl, through the sunny morning weather.
A handsome couple they made; & as they walked through the
Hôtel garden together, a Russian princess, who was taking an
early airing, observed to her little French secretary: "that those
English were fiancées; she could see it." As they reached the
gate, a little child who was racing after a hoop, stumbled & fell
crying across their path; & Madeline stooped down & picked
him up very tenderly. "Are you hurt?" "Not very much,
Madame," said the child; & Madeline felt the blood flying into
her face, & wondered whether Guy were very much vexed at
having her mistaken for his wife. On through the sunny morning weather: who can tell of that walk, with all its pretty little
incidents, & surprises & adventures? It was such a pastoral as
drops now & then between the tragedies & farces of life.
Madeline was perfectly happy; & if Guy was not as happy as
she, he was in a better mood than he had been for many a day,
& the bright morning air, the beautiful scenery, the sweet
English face at his side, warmed him more & more into hearty
enjoyment. As they walked, the flower-basket was filled with
new trophies; & when they reached their destination, Guy

spread Madeline's shawl under a nut-tree, & sat down by her side to sketch. "Why not take a drawing lesson today?" he said, as she watched him pointing his pencils & making his slight preparations. "I think one could learn anything in such beautiful weather." "I had rather watch you," said Madeline, "& you know I have to arrange my flowers too. Oh, what a beautiful day!" "Perfect. I didn't know what an attractive little nook Interlaken is before." "And you are going tomorrow?" asked Madeline, dropping her lashes. "I think so. Every artist is at heart a wanderer—begging Pope's pardon for taking such a liberty with his line. There, Miss Graham, what do you think of those outlines?" "How quick you are! Oh, how cleverly you have done it." Guy laughed. "Such injudicious praise as yours would soon spoil me," he said. "I suppose so," Madeline returned naively. "You know I am so ignorant." Guy went on with his sketch; he revelled in the deep, luxurious Summer silence, the whisper of the leaves above his head, the easy consciousness that if he did lift his eyes from his work they would meet nothing less in harmony with the radiant day than Madeline Graham's fair, sweet face bent above her flowers. Now & then, as the sketch grew beneath his quick pencil, she offered her shy criticism or her shyer praise; but for the most part they were silent, as though afraid by word or movement to break the spell of peacefulness that had fallen upon them. It was not until they had again reached the gate of the Hôtel garden, that either reverted to Guy's coming departure. "I am glad that our last walk has been so pleasant," he said. "I wonder how many more walks you will take after I am gone." "You are really going?" He saw the colour creep upwards, & the long lashes tremble. "I had intended to go," he answered, leaning against the gate. "I suppose—I suppose it has grown dull," murmured Madeline. "It has grown so pleasant that I wish I had not reached my limit," said Guy. "When a man proposes to spend two days at a place, & lengthens his visit to nearly two weeks, as I have done, he must begin to consider how much time he has left for the rest of his tour." "We shall miss you," ventured Madeline, overwhelmed with blushes. "Papa, I mean, will . . ." "Won't *you* miss me?" said Guy, very low. Madeline's half-averted cheek turned a deeper crimson; her heart was beating stormily, & everything seemed to swim before her. "I don't know," she whispered, tremblingly. In any other person, at any other time, such an answer would have been bête; in Madeline Graham, with the sunset light striking her pale golden braids, & the church-bells coming softly through the sweet evening air, as they stood by the gate, it seemed to Guy Hastings very sweet & musical. "If I thought you would miss me I should be almost glad to go," he said, quietly. "And yet, I do not know why I go. It is so peaceful here, that I feel as if life were worth a little—if I go, I shall probably do my best to tumble down a ravine." Madeline lifted her blue eyes in wonderment; she had never heard him speak so before. "Yes," he went on, "You do not know what it is to feel that everything is worthless & heartless, as I have done. I envy you. I almost wish that I were going to stay here." He paused; &, moved by the weary sadness which his voice & words had for the first time betrayed, Madeline gathered heart to say, holding out her hand: "I don't understand, but I am very sorry for you. You must have had a disappointment. Stay here." And Guy stayed; why not? As he had said, life seemed worth a little in this friendly atmosphere of peace, & in

Madeline's society. An inexpressible charm, which he scarcely acknowledged to himself, made her society pleasant; the quiet, Arcadian days were an utter contrast to the dash & hurry of his unsatisfied life; he had found a palmtree in the desert-sand & he sat down to rest. As for Madeline, on the day when she met Guy in the covered bridge, that mysterious thing called "love at first sight" had entered in & taken possession of her heart. His manner had, indeed, a great fascination for all; & he was unusually gentle & serious with Madeline; then he was handsome, & Madeline, though she was not, like her Papa, a judge of art, had the good taste common to most girls, to admire a handsome face. As for those words of his by the gate, to say that she was a woman is to say that they aroused her sympathy & admiration as nothing else could have done, & raised Guy into a suffering hero. Nothing could be purer & more childlike than Madeline's passion; it blent with her life like a strain of sweet music, in which as yet there were no jarring chords; there was nothing noisy or turbulent about it. So the Summer stole on through balmy days & short, warm nights; Guy lingered at Interlaken, & Madeline saw him daily. He certainly treated her with marked admiration, & both Mr. & Mrs. Graham were not slow to draw their conclusions therefrom; but he spoke no word of love, &, as the happy days passed, seemed inclined to remain "half her lover, all her friend." Nor did Madeline feel the want of a closer appeal to her heart. The present was all-sufficient. Why should this pastoral ever end, or if it was to end, why should she not enjoy it the more fully now? Her love for Guy was as yet almost too idealized & abstract to demand a reciprocation. Enough that he was by her side, & that he was glad to be there. Mr. Graham, too, was quite easy on the subject. Madeline was a pretty girl, & Hastings was evidently very much gone on her; he was of good family & she had money enough for both; no match could be more desirable, & none seemed more likely to prosper. It was natural that they should like to spin out their courtship-days; young people have the whole world before them, & are never in a hurry. But Mrs. Graham was not so well-pleased with the turn affairs had taken. "Don't be so confident, John," she said, anxiously. "I had rather trust Maddy with a good, honest business man than one of these fine, fast young fellows. Very likely he is only amusing himself; what does he want with a merchant's daughter? No, no; it will come to nothing & if it goes on much longer the child's heart will be broken. I have heard stories enough about Mr. Hastings & his set, & I don't believe in one of them!" "Nonsense!" said Mr. Graham, angrily. He had set his heart on the match & these warnings of his wife's, which he could not in his heart despise, made him uneasy.

Chap. XI. The End of the Season.

"Adieu, bal, plaisir, amour! On disait: Pauvre Constance!
Et on dansait jusqu'au Jour chez l'ambassadeur de France."
Delavigne.

ON A CERTAIN EVENING near the close of those busy, rushing
summer months which Londoners call "the season," Lady
Breton was sitting alone in the long, luxurious dressing-room
which opened off her satin-hung boudoir. She wore one of
those mysterious combinations of lace & ribands & soft folds
called a wrapper, & as she leaned back rather wearily in her
deep-arm-chair, her slippered feet were stretched out to meet
the glow of the small wood-fire crackling on the hearth. There
was no other light in the room, but the fire-flash, unless a certain dull twilight gleam through the dark folds of the curtains,
deserves such a name; for my lady had given orders not to be
disturbed, adding that she would ring for the lamps. But in
the soft, flickering of the flames, that rose & fell fitfully, it
was a very white & mournful face that sank back in the shadow
of the crimson cushion; a face in which there was no discernible
trace of the rosy, audacious Georgie Rivers whom we used to
know. Nor was it the splendid, resistless Lady Breton who had
taken London by storm that Summer; but only a very miserable little personage, occasionally breaking the twilight hush
of the warm room with a heavy, aching cough, that made her

lean shivering nearer the pleasant blaze. In fact, Georgie had at last broken down, in body & mind, under the weight of her bitter mistake; which all her triumphs & her petty glories seemed only to make bitterer, with a sense of something empty & unsatisfied, lower than the surface-gayety of the ball-room. The pang had deepened & deepened, driving her farther into the ceaseless rush of society with the main hope of losing her individual sorrow there; no one was gayer than Lady Breton. But at home, in the grand house, with its grave servants & its pictures & treasures, that was no more hope of forgetting than abroad. Any sympathy that might eventually have grown up between the old lord & his young wife, had been frozen by Georgie's persistent indifference to him; & whatever love his worn-out old heart had at first lavished on her, was lost in the nearer interests of a good dinner or an amusing play. Lord Breton, in short, relapsed entirely into his bachelor-habits, & was only with his wife, or conscious of her existence when she presided at his table, or entered a ball-room at his side. He was not ungenerous; he allowed her plenty of liberty & still had a comfortable pleasure in feeling that he was the possessor of the most charming woman in London—but day by day, she became less a part of his life. And still at her heart clung the love that she had despised of old, & whose unconquerable reality she was learning now—too late. Jack Egerton's reproaches seemed to have been the last drop in her cup of shame & bitterness—again & again came the wretched, haunting thought that she had lost Guy's esteem forever, & nothing could win back the place in his heart that she had sold so cheap. So she mused on in the closing darkness, over the fire-light, & it was 8 o'clock when she rang for her maid, who came in with the lamps & a bottle of cough-syrup for my lady. Georgie rose wearily from her seat, drawing a soft shawl close about her shoulders; &, as the maid stood waiting for orders, said between her painful coughing: "I shall dress for the ball now, Sidenham." "But, my lady," the woman answered, "you have had no dinner." "No, I did not want any, thanks. It is time to dress." "But—my lady," persisted the maid, "your cough is so bad . . . indeed, my lady . . ." Georgie interrupted her with an impatient movement. "My white dress, Sidenham. Have the flowers come home?" "Yes, my lady." And the process of the toilette began. Sidenham had a real attachment for her mistress, but she knew that my lady could brook no questioning of her will, & being a good servant, went about her duty obediently. Lord Breton had dined out that evening, but at about 9.30, as Sidenham was putting the last touches to Georgie's hair, he knocked unexpectedly at the dressing-room door, & then came in, in his evening dress. "I hoped you were in bed by—good Heavens!" he exclaimed, as Georgie rose in her glistening satin. "You don't mean to say that you are going out tonight?" Sidenham, shaking out my lady's train, looked volumes of sympathy at my lord. "Oh, certainly," returned Georgie, unconcernedly. "It is the Duchess of Westmoreland's ball tonight, you know." "But this is madness—madness. Your cough was much worse today—such exposure at night would be extremely dangerous." Georgie was clasping her diamonds, with her back turned towards him, & merely shrugged her white shoulders slightly. "Let me dissuade you," Lord Breton continued, with real anxiety. "Surely it is little to forfeit one ball—the last of the season—for one's health's sake. Your physician would certainly not advise such imprudence, such abso-

lute risk." "Very likely," said Georgie, nonchalantly, "but
—'when the cat's away the mice will play,' you know." "I
know that going out tonight would be folly on your part; let
me beg you to desist from it." "My white fan, Sidenham. I
presume," said Georgie, turning to face her husband as she
spoke, "that I shall have your escort?" "I am going to the
ball." "And yet" she continued lightly, "you wish to exile me
from it? I should die of ennui in half an hour alone here!"
"Then—then, may I offer you my company?" he said, eagerly,
taking the cloak from Sidenham's hands. "Let us give up the
ball, Georgina." Georgie was really moved; such a demonstra-
tion was so unusual on Lord Breton's part, that it could not
fail to touch her. But it was not her rôle to shew this. "No indeed!" she replied, clasping her bracelet, & coming closer to
him. "Why should either of us be sacrificed? Instead of suicide
for one, it would be—murder for both! Please put my cloak
on." "You go then?" said Lord Breton, coldly, with a gathering
frown. "Oh, yes. As you say, it is the last ball of the season.
Tomorrow I shall do penance." And drawing her cloak close,
with a suppressed cough, she swept out of the room. The
Duchess of Westmoreland's ball, at Lochiel House, was a very
grand & a very brilliant affair, & a very fitting finale to one
of the gayest seasons that people could recall. Everybody (that
is, as her Grace expressively said, "everybody that is anybody")
was there; & the darling of the night was, as usual, the fascinating Lady Breton. White as her white dress, unrelieved by
a shade of colour, she came in on her husband's arm; people
remembered afterwards, how strangely, deadly pale she was.
But she danced continually, talked & laughed with everyone
more graciously than ever, & raised the hearts of I don't know

how many desponding lovers by her charming gayety & good-nature. She was resting after the last quadrille, when the Duke of Westmoreland himself, came up to her, with the inexpressibly relieved air of a model host who, having done his duty by all the ugly dowagers in the room, finds himself at liberty to follow his own taste for a few moments. "I don't think" he said, answering Georgie's greeting "that you have seen the Duchess's new conservatories. Will you let me be your cicerone?" "How did you guess, Duke," she returned, gaily "that I was longing to escape from the heat & light? Do take me, if I am not carrying you off from any more—agreeable—duty!" "My duty is over," said the Duke, smiling. "But you are coughing tonight, Lady Breton, & I cannot allow you to go into the cooler air without a wrap." Signing to a servant, he sent for a soft fur mantle, & having folded it carefully about Georgie's shoulders, led her on his arm through the long & brilliant suites. Followed by many an envious & many an admiring eye, she walked on with her proud step, talking lightly & winningly to her noble escort, until they reached the folding doors of the great conservatories. The Duke led her in, & they paused on the threshold looking down the green vista of gorgeous tropical plants. The gay dance-music came like a soft echo from the distant ball-room, mingling with the clear tinkle of fountains that tossed their spray amid the branching ferns & palm-trees on which the Chinese lanterns swung from the ceiling, shed an unreal, silvery glow. For a moment neither spoke; then Georgie looked up at her host with a bright smile. "Fairyland!" she exclaimed. "No one shall persuade me that this is the work of anyone less ethereal than Queen Mab herself! Is it real? Will it last?" "I hope so," his Grace answered, laughing; "it would be a pity that her Elfin Majesty's work should vanish in a single night." "Only, as children say, 'it is too good to be true,'" said Georgie, merrily. "At least, to us lesser mortals, who are not accustomed to all the marvels of Lochiel House." "Will you come on a little further?" said the Duke, well-pleased. "I want to shew you some rare ferns. Here they are." And so they passed along the aisle of mingled green, in the soft moonlike radiance; pausing here & there to admire or discuss the Duke's favourite specimens. At the end of the long, cool bower a broad ottoman stood in a recess filled with ferns; & Georgie asked to sit down before entering the next conservatory. "You are tiring yourself, Lady Breton?" asked the Duke, anxiously, sitting down beside her, & drawing the mantle, which had slipped down, over her shoulder. "No, not tired, indeed," she answered, "but half dizzy with so much beauty. I must sit still to be able to enjoy it perfectly—sit still, & drink it in." "It is a relief after the crowded rooms," assented his Grace. "I was longing to be here all the evening." "I cannot wonder. Do you know, Duke," said Georgie, laughing, "if I were disposed to be sentimental I should say that I envied the gardener who has these conservatories in charge more than anyone in Lochiel House!" The Duke echoed her laugh. "If it suits you to be sentimental just now, Lady Breton, the gardener—an old protégé of mine—is a very fit subject. He has a romance attached to him." "Better & better!" cried Georgie. "He can come in here & dream of it!" "I daresay though—poor fellow!—he would rather forget it," said the Duke. Georgie started slightly, & a strange look came into her eyes. "Oh, if we could but forget," she half-whispered; then, in a different tone: "but what of the gardener? I will not let you off with

that story; you must play Princess Scheherazade, Duke!"
"Most obediently, though poor Watson probably never intended his poor little love-affair to serve such a grand purpose.
Well—'anything, but to the purpose' is my motto, Lady Breton, so here is the whole romance. Watson came into my
father's service as a lad & rose to be one of the undergardeners
down at Morley Towers. There he wooed my mother's maid,
a pretty young woman, who in the end spoiled two lives by
her ambition.—Are you ill, Lady Breton?" "No, no," said
Georgie, hastily, playing nervously with her bouquet, "please
go on. I am quite impatient." "Watson," continued the Duke,
"was successful in his suit, & the wedding was arranged, much
to the poor fellow's happiness—for he was as genuinely in
love, Lady Breton," said the Duke, with slight sarcasm, "as any
gentleman would have been—the wedding, I say, was arranged, when my father brought home a fine French valet,
who got a larger salary, & had altogether a higher seat in the
synagogue, than Watson. The bride, whose head was turned
by the attentions of this more fascinating rival, gave Watson
the slip—jilted him, and—great Heavens! You are faint, Lady
Breton—what is it?" The bouquet had slipped from Georgie's
powerless hands, & she could scarcely answer, as the Duke
bent over her, "it will be over—in a moment—" "Let me call
someone," said his Grace, anxiously; but she shook her head,
& whispered faintly, "No, no . . . Do not call . . . it will be
over . . ." "I will get you some wine. Can you wait here alone?"
She gave a little, frightened cry & caught his hand wildly.
"Don't leave me! I . . . I . . . am better . . . now. I don't want
anything . . . Take me away, Duke!" Sorely perplexed, he
helped her to rise, & giving her his arm, led her very slowly

back through the conservatory. She had evidently rallied her strength for the effort, for though she did not trust herself to speak, her step was almost steady; & at last, to the Duke's intense relief, they reached the doors. The room on which the conservatory opened was hung with pictures & during the earlier part of the evening had been deserted for the other end of the suite; but the crowd had taken a new turn now & people were thronging in, to fill the interval before supper. Once or twice in his anxious progress through the crush the Duke was arrested, & not a few astonished glances met Lady Breton's white, suffering face; but they had nearly gained a door leading by a back way to the cloak-room, when his Grace felt the cold hand slip from his arm, & Georgie fell backward fainting. In an instant they were ringed in by a startled, eager crowd; but the Duke, lifting the slight, unconscious form in his arms, refused peremptorily all offers for assistance, & despatching a messenger for Lord Breton, himself carried Georgie into a dressing-room, out of reach of the bustle & curiosity of his officious guests.

Chap. XII.   Poor Teresina.

"When pain & anguish wring the brow, a ministering Angel thou!"
Scott: "Marmion."

THE RETURNING WINTER found Guy Hastings again at
Rome, in the old studio which he & Egerton had shared the
year before; but Jack was still in England, though he wrote in
the expectancy of joining his Telemachus in the early Spring.
Meanwhile Guy, on settling down in his Winter quarters, began to apply himself with real assiduity to his art. He painted
a successful picture which was bought by an Italian connois-
seur; & inspirited by this piece of good fortune, grew more &
more attached to the great work he had heretofore treated as
play. He had lost his utter recklessness in this deepening interest, & a new & softening influence seemed to have entered
into his imbittered life since the happy weeks at Interlaken.
This influence was not the less tender or pleasant that it was
somehow connected with a pair [of] sweet, childlike blue eyes
& a low voice full of shy music. Little did Madeline, cherishing
the secret of her first love in silence, guess the innocent change
she had worked in her hero; & perhaps Guy himself scarcely
realized her quiet power. When the Grahams came back to
Rome however, the intercourse which had charmed the Interlaken days, was renewed; Guy was always welcomed in their
apartment, & many a little breakfast or supper was given in

their honour in his sunny studio. Mr. Graham, too, discovered that Madeline's portrait must be painted; & twice a week she & her mother would knock at Guy's door, until, when the last coat of varnish was dry & the picture sent home, he grew to miss the timid rap & the pleasant hour that ensued & to discover that it had been, unconsciously, the brightest part of his day. Madeline's frail health grew stronger, & her shy laugh gayer; & though one parent was far from satisfied with the cause, both could not but rejoice over the effect of this change. Altogether, the Winter was a happy, if a quiet one to the few with whom our story is most concerned; & as the days slipped by, they forged the imperceptible links of interest & sympathy which were drawing Guy nearer to Madeline. One of these links was brought about by a little personage who by this time had nearly dropped out of Guy's remembrance, although her face was reflected on more than one canvas hung upon his studio wall. He was hurrying homeward near dusk on a soft day toward the end of January, & taking a short cut to the Piazza ———, struck a little, out of the way street, apparently quite deserted in the waning light. The houses were old & ruinous, & if Guy had found time to pause, their tumbling picturesqueness would have delighted his artist-eye; but as it was, he was in too great haste to notice anything, until at a turn in the street he nearly stumbled across a little drooping figure huddled against a broken flight of steps. Bending down in astonishment, he asked in Italian what was the matter. There was no answer, or movement, & he repeated his question more anxiously. Just then a coarse-faced woman came swinging down the street bare-headed, & paused in astonishment to see the handsome Signore Inglese bending over a little, cowering contadina with her face hidden. "Eh, she won't move, Signore," said the woman, grinning. "She's been there these three hours." "Is she dead?" asked Guy, pityingly. "Dead? Santa Maria! No, not she. Maybe she is crazy." "You cannot leave her here," said Guy; "if she is alive she should be taken in somewhere." The woman shrugged her shoulders. "I tell you, she won't move. I don't know who she is." "Poverina!" said Guy, very low; but he had scarcely spoken when a tremor shot through the crouching form at his feet, & a faint little cry reached him. "Signore—it is Teresina!" "Teresina," repeated Guy in amazement. "Are you ill? What is the matter?" "Eh," said the woman, staring, "The Signore knows her, then?" "What has happened?" Guy continued, as a burst of sobs answered his questions. "Will you get up, Teresina, & let me carry you into some house?" But she did not lift her hidden face, nor move from her cowering attitude. Guy was in sore perplexity. He could not leave her, not knowing whether she was ill or frightened in some way; & the woman who had been watching him with an expression of sleepy surprise on her heavy face ran off here in pursuit of a brown-legged little boy who was scampering toward the Piazza. Just then, as Guy was gazing doubtfully down the crooked street, two people appeared moving quickly against the dark sunset glow; one a short, plain-faced little woman, with the indefinable air of an English servant—the other tall, & blonde, with soft blue eyes & her hands full of flowers. "Miss Graham!" exclaimed Guy, as she recognized him with a start & a deepening blush. "What is the matter?" said Madeline, glancing with surprise towards Teresina while Priggett, the maid, hung back with a disapproving stare. "Who is that poor creature, Mr. Hastings?

Why," she continued suddenly, "it must be your little peasant
—Teresina!" "So it is," said Guy, "& I cannot find whether she
is ill or only unhappy. She will not move, & I cannot get her to
answer my questions." "Poor thing!" and Madeline, regardless
of the dirty cobble-stones & her own soft, pretty dress, knelt
down beside Teresina; & began to speak in her sweet, shy Italian. "Will you not tell us if you are suffering?" she said; "we
are so sorry for you & we cannot leave you here." "Miss—" said
Priggett in an agony, "Miss, it's growing very dark." "Never
mind, Priggett. Mr. Hastings, will you hold these flowers,
please?" & putting her roses into his hand, she quietly slipped
her arm about Teresina & raised the poor little drooping head
tenderly. "I do not think she is in pain—speak to her, Mr.
Hastings." Guy bent over her & said a few soothing words; &
Madeline, still kneeling by her side, asked again very gently:
"What is it, Teresina?" "Tell the Signora," urged Guy. "She
is very kind & wants to help you." Teresina was still sobbing,
but less violently & now she made no attempt to hide her face;
& in a few moments they caught a little, trembling answer.
"I am hungry." "Poor thing—poor thing—" said Madeline,
through her tears. "Have you no home?" She gave a little
shriek & tried to hide her face, repeating passionately "No, no,
no!" "She is not fit to answer any questions," said Madeline.
"Mr. Hastings, she must be carried into some house at once &
taken care of." The woman who had stared at Guy came back
just then from her chase to the piazza; & calling her, they per-
suaded her to let Teresina be taken into her house close by.
Guy lifted the poor, fainting creature in his arms & Madeline
followed, for once regardless of Priggett's indignant glances,
while the woman led the way up some tumbling steps into a

wretched little room. The night had fallen when, having left some money & sundry directions, they turned once more into the lonely street, Madeline shyly accepting Guy's escort home. "I will go & see the poor thing tomorrow," she said, her sweet voice full of pity. "I think she has had a great blow. She does not seem really ill—only exhausted." "She could not be under kinder care—poor child!" said Guy, thoughtfully. "I cannot understand what has happened. She was happily married to her lover last year—as you know." "He may have died. How lonely she seemed! O poor, poor thing—it makes me feel almost guilty to think how loved & happy I am while others . . ." Madeline brushed away her tears hastily, & for a few moments neither spoke. The next morning found Priggett & her young mistress hurrying down the same obscure street, laden with baskets & shawls, towards the house into which Teresina had been carried. She was still lying on the low bed where they had left her the night before, her great eyes wide with grief, her childish face haggard with lines of suffering. "She won't eat much, Signora," said Giovita, the woman of the house, as Madeline bent anxiously over the bed, "but I think she'll be better soon, poor fanciulla!" Teresina turned her eyes to the fair, pitying face that stooped above her. "You are the beautiful Signora," she whispered, "that came to me last night. The Signore Inglese said you would be kind." Madeline's colour brightened softly; he called her kind! "I want to be your friend, Teresina," she answered; "for he has told me a great deal about you, & we are both so sorry for you!" Teresina sighed. A new contentment was entering into her eyes as they met those other eyes, pure & tender as a guardian Angel's. "You look like one of the Saints in the great pictures," she murmured dreamily.

83

"It was at Easter—I saw it—the saint with the white face like yours." "Never mind that, Teresina," Madeline said gently. "I want you to tell me why you were so hungry & unhappy & all alone in the street last night. Do not be afraid to tell me. If you have no friends, I want to help you & take care of you." "I have no friends," Teresina whispered, still gazing up at Madeline. "Oh, I am so unhappy, Signora . . . I ran away to starve all alone . . . I could not kill myself . . ." she shuddered & hid her face with a burst of sobs. At first Madeline could win no more from her, but gradually, as she sat by the wretched bedside, she learned the story of Teresina's sorrow. She had been married—poor child!—to her sweetheart, Matteo, & they had been so happy, until Matteo could get no work, & grew harsh & reckless. Teresina was unhappy, & cried because he did not love her any more—& the bambino died of the fever, & Matteo got worse & worse. Still there was no work, & Teresina was ill at home—Matteo said he could not feed her. He used to go out all day, & one day he did not come back— she never saw him again, & she knew that he had deserted her. "Oh, it was so lonely without the bambino," ended the poor little wife, through her tears. "I could not bear to go home, for the Madre is dead & the Padre was so angry when I married Matteo—& I did not want anything but to run away & hide my-self—& die." But she did not die; Madeline felt a new interest in her after this & watched & comforted her tenderly; & in a few days she was strong enough to be moved from the wretched house to the Graham's apartment. They sent for her father, a rough old peasant who would have nothing to do with her, & cursed her for marrying against his will. Teresina begged with passionate tears not to go back to him; & Madeline had

grown so attached to her that she easily prevailed on her father
to keep the poor child at least for the present. On Teresina's
part there had sprung up a blind adoration of the beautiful
Signorina who was the Signore Inglese's friend; she asked
nothing but to stay with her always & serve her & follow her
like a dog. Guy was not a little interested in the fate of his poor
little model; & Madeline's kindness to her won him more &
more. Few girls, he thought, would have behaved as nobly, as
impulsively & as tenderly as Madeline had done. And so it was
that Teresina's misfortune revealed to him the earnest, quiet
beauty of this shy English girl's character, & made him think
more & more seriously every day that in this world of sin &
folly & darkness there are after all some pure spirits moving,
like sun-gleams in a darkened chamber.

Chap. XIII.   Villa Doria-Pamfili.

"If thou canst reason, sure thou dost not love." *Old Play.*

ON ONE OF THOSE delicious languid days of Spring that follow in the footsteps of the short Roman Winter, the Grahams
drove out to spend a long afternoon at the Villa Doria-Pamfili,
where the violets & anemones were awake in every hollow, &
the trees putting on their tenderest silver-green. Guy rode by
the side of the carriage, having breakfasted that morning with
its occupants & engaged to join them again in the afternoon.
Day by day Madeline's society had grown sweeter & more
needful to him, her soft presence effacing as nothing else could
the bitter past. Great sorrows cast long shadows; & in reality
the gloom of his disappointed love still hung darkly over
Hastings' life; but it was a softened gloom when he was at
Madeline's side, losing his heart-loneliness in her sunny companionship. When a man marries without falling in love he
always has at hand an elaborate course of reasoning to prove
beyond all doubt the advisableness of the step he takes; & some
such process was occupying Guy's thoughts as he trotted along
on his chesnut, Rienzi, beside the Grahams' carriage. Since his
engagement had been broken he had, as we have said, felt all
hope & interest in life slipping away from his empty grasp; &
now that he had met & known Madeline it struck him with
what renewed dreariness he would return to his old, reckless

ways when their paths divided. More than once he had dreamed of his motley studio with a fair figure moving continually about it, or a soft, flushed face bending over him as he worked; & had wondered if life would not get a new zest with some- one beside him to be cherished & worked for until death. Madeline's peculiar innocence & shy simplicity had soothed him in contrast to the gay, wilful charms with which his most cruel recollections were united; he thought that here was a shrinking, clinging creature who would need his tender pro- tection & look up to him always for the help & love that another had despised. In short, on that sweet Spring afternoon, the impressions & reflections of the whole Winter had nearly resolved themselves into a determination to ask Madeline for his wife, when the whole party reached the gates of the Villa Doria. Giving Rienzi over to his groom, Guy stood by the car- riage to help Madeline & her mother out; & then they all strolled along through the beautiful princely grounds. Made- line's passion for flowers was very pretty that day; prettier than ever it seemed to Hastings, as she bent down to fill her hands with violets, or ran on in search of a new blossom under the greening boughs. Oh, the sunshiny peacefulness of that long Spring afternoon, under the soft Italian sky, with the wood-flowers underfoot & the tree-branches closing above, bubbling over with the earliest bird-music of the new-drest year! They wandered on in the delicious Spring-time idleness that had fallen upon them all; now & then resting on a bench in some quiet alley or soft, violet-sown slope, or pausing to ad- mire a beautiful view—all forgetting that even in the Villa Doria-Pamfili, on a Heavenly day of Spring, the hours will fly & the sun stoop to the west. Strolling along by Madeline's side, carrying her sunshade & her cloak, Guy recalled Robert Spencer's bright words: "How lightly falls the foot of Time That only treads on flowers!" He repeated them to her, adding as he glanced down at his feet, "literally true here, is it not, Miss Graham? You trample a violet at every step." "Oh, I am so sorry for them!" said Madeline, earnestly; "but what can I do? My hands are quite full." She was standing still, in her floating white dress, framed by rising boughs, & holding a great mass of the balmy purple treasures. Guy Hastings had never seen a fairer picture in a fairer setting. "If I had my pallette & canvas here, Miss Graham, I should paint you as you stand, for a Proserpine." "I am glad you haven't then," returned Madeline, laughing, "for I should be longing to escape in search of some more flowers, & how tired I should get, standing so long." "You will be tired now if you don't rest a little," said Guy. They were standing near an old grey stone bench, hidden in tree-shadows, with a cushioning of deep moss & anemones around it. "Let us sit down, Miss Graham," he continued. "You are dropping your violets at every step & my practical mind suggests that they should be tied together to prevent further loss." Madeline laughed, & sat down while he quietly folded her cloak about her, & then took his place at her side. Mr. and Mrs. Graham had walked on slowly, & were presently lost among the trees; but neither Guy nor Madeline noticed this—which is perhaps scarcely surprising. It suited Hastings very well to be sitting there, holding the violets, while Madeline's soft hands took them from him one by one & bound them carefully together; he had never found her quite so lovely as on that golden afternoon. "Am I to have none as a reward for my help?" he asked, as she took the last violets to add to her bunch. "You are very miserly with your treasures, Miss Graham." "Because I don't think you love them as well as I do," she said, smiling. "But you did hold them very well, & here is your reward." She handed him two or three, with her soft blush, & he was very near kissing the white ungloved hand that offered them. But reflecting that so sudden a proceeding might startle his shy damsel, & break up the sweet, idle course of their tête à tête, he wisely refrained, & only thanked her as he put the violets in his coat. "I shall wear them as my Legion of honour," he added, smiling. "But they will fade so soon! Do you know," said Madeline, glancing up into the handsome blue eyes bent on her face, & then looking quickly downward with a blush, as if she had read some secret there too subtle to be put into words—"do you know, it always makes me a little sad—foolishly, I suppose—to gather flowers, when I think of that." "Gather ye roses while ye may!" hummed Guy, laughing. "I don't think the flowers are to be pitied, Miss Graham." "Why not?" said Madeline, very low. "Why not? Because— I put myself in their place & judge their feelings by—my own." Madeline's heart beat quicker, & she sprang up suddenly. "Where is Papa, Mr. Hastings? I think . . ." Guy caught her hand. "Stay, Miss Graham," he said as she rose. "Before you go, I want to say a few words to you. Will you hear me?" He led her quietly back to her shady seat, & sat down beside her again, leaning forward to catch sight of her half-turned face & dropped lashes. "I do not know," he went on, in his low, winning voice, "what right I have to say these words, or to expect an answer; for I feel, day by day, as I watch you, so young, so happy, so beautiful—pardon me—I feel how little I can give in return for what your kindness has encouraged me to ask."

He spoke with a calm grave gentleness as far removed from the anxious, entangled faltering of a lover as if he had been offering friendly criticism or long-prepared advice. Madeline's only answer was the rising crimson on her cheek; & he continued, in the same quiet, undisturbed tones: "I told you once that there was little interest or happiness left in my life—a wasted life I fear it has been!—but since I have known you, Miss Graham, it has seemed as though an Angel were beckoning me back to a new existence—a more peaceful one than I have ever known." He paused. His eyes had wandered from the flushed face at his side to the golden streaks of sunset barring the soft Western sky. It seemed to Madeline as if the wild, hot beating of her heart must drown her voice; she could not speak. "You know—you must know—" he said presently, "how miserably little I have to offer—the battered remains of a misspent life! Heaven forbid that I should claim the same right as another man to this little hand, (let me hold it). Heaven forbid that I should call myself worthy of the answer I have dared to hope for!" She had half-risen again, with a faint attempt to free her hand; but he rose also, & quietly drew her closer. "Madeline, can you guess that I want to ask you to be my wife?" He had possession of both her hands, & she did not struggle but only stood before him with eyes downcast & burning cheeks. "Will you give me no answer, Madeline?" he said, gently. There was a faint movement of her tremulous lips, & bending down he caught a soft, fluttering "Yes." He lifted her right hand to his lips & for a moment neither spoke. Then Madeline said, in a frightened, half-guilty voice, "Oh, let us go to Papa." "They are coming to us," returned Guy, still detaining her, as he caught sight of Mr. & Mrs. Graham moving slowly towards them under the shadowy ilex-clumps. "Why do you want to run away from me, Madeline? I have the right to call you so now, have I not?" "Yes," she murmured, still not daring to meet his kind, searching eyes. "But, come, please, let us go & meet them. I . . . I must tell Mamma, you know . . ." "One moment. I have another right also, dear one!" He stooped & kissed her quickly as he spoke, then drawing her trembling hand through his arm, led her forward to the advancing couple under the trees. Madeline's tearful confusion alone would have betrayed everything to her mother's quick eyes. "Oh, Mamma, Mamma," she cried, running to Mrs. Graham & hiding her face. Guy came up, in his quiet easy way, looking frankly into the mother's rosy, troubled face. "I have asked Madeline to be my wife," he said, "& she has consented." "Maddy, Maddy," cried Mrs. Graham, tearfully, "is it so, my dear?" But Mr. Graham was disposed to view things more cheerfully, & while the mother & daughter were weeping in each other's arms, shook Hastings' hand with ill-concealed delight. "She is our only one, Hastings, & we could not trust you with a dearer thing, but—there, I won't exactly say 'No'!" "Believe me," Guy returned, "I know how precious is the treasure I have dared to ask for. I shall try to make myself worthy of her by guarding her more tenderly than my own life—if indeed you consent. . . ." Madeline turned a shy, appealing glance at Mr. Graham as she stood clinging to her mother. "Eh, Maddy?" said the merchant, goodnaturedly, "what can the old father say, after all? Well—I don't know how to refuse. We must think, we must think." "Madeline," said Hastings, bending over her, "will you take my arm to the carriage?" They did not say much as they walked along in the dying sunset light;

but a pleasant sense of possessorship came over Guy as he felt the shy hand lying on his arm—& who can sum up the wealth of Madeline's silent happiness? And so they passed through the gates, & the Spring twilight fell over Villa Doria-Pamfili.

Chap. XIV. Left Alone.

"Death, like a robber, crept in unaware."
Old Play. (From the Spanish)

THREE SLOW WEEKS of illness followed Georgie's imprudence at Lochiel House; & in September when she began to
grow a little better, she was ordered off to the Mediterranean
for the Winter. She scarcely regretted this; the trip in Lord
Breton's yacht would be pleasant, & any change of scene welcome for a time—but as far as her health was concerned, she
cared very little for its preservation, since life in every phase
grew more hopelessly weary day by day. Favourable winds
made their passage short & smooth, but when they reached the
Mediterranean Georgie was too poorly to enjoy the short
cruise along its coast which had been planned, & they made
directly for Nice. After a few dreary days of suffering at a
Hôtel, Lord Breton gave up all idea of prolonging his yachting
& by his physician's advice moved at once into a small sunny
villa where Georgie could have perfect quiet for several
months. She was very ill again, & it was long before she re-
covered from the exhaustion of the journey. Even when she
began to grow better & lie on her lounge or creep downstairs,
it was a cheerless household; for Lord Breton, cut off by re-
curring attacks of gout from any exercise or amusement that
the town might have afforded, grew daily more irritable &

gloomy. Nor did Georgie attempt at first to rouse herself for his sake; it was hard enough, she thought, to be shut up forever face to face with her own unquenchable sorrow & remorse. It did not occur to her that wherever her heart might be, her duty lay with her husband. She learned this one March day, as we do learn all our great heart-lessons, suddenly & plainly. Her physician had been to see her, & in taking leave said very gravely: "in truth, Lady Breton, I am just now more anxious about your husband's welfare than your own. He suffers a great deal, & needs constant distraction. You will excuse my saying, frankly, that I think the loneliness, the want of—may I say sympathy? in his life, is preying upon him heavily. I cannot tell you to be easy, where I see such cause for anxiety." These words—grave & direct, as a good physician's always are—affected Georgie strangely. Could it be that he too suffered, & felt a bitter want in his life? she questioned herself. Could it be that she had failed in her duty? that something more was demanded of her? And with this there came over her with a great rush, the thought of her own selfish absorption & neglect. Had he not, after all, tried to be a kind & a generous husband? Had she not repulsed him over & over again? In that hour of sad self-conviction the first unselfish tears that had ever wet her cheek sprang to Georgie Breton's eyes. Remorse had taken a new & a more practical form with her. For once she saw how small, how base & petty had been her part in the great, harmonious drama of life; how mean the ends for which she had made so great a sacrifice; how childish the anger & disappointment she had cherished—how self-made the fate against which she had railed. She had looked forward that day to a drive, the chief pleasure & excitement of her monotonous hours; but ringing the bell, she countermanded her carriage, & went downstairs to her husband's room. Lord Breton was sitting helpless in his arm-chair, the sun dazzling his eyes through the unshaded window, & his newspapers pushed aside as if whatever interest they contained had long ago been exhausted. He looked up with some surprise when Georgie entered with her slow, feeble step, & crossing the room quietly dropped the Venetian shade. "Thank you," he said. "The sun was blinding. I hope you are feeling better to-day, Georgina?" "Oh, yes, I think so," she returned with a brave effort at gaiety, as she sank down in a low chair. "But I am afraid you are suffering. I . . . I am awfully sorry." Lord Breton's amazement waxed stronger. He even forgave the slang in which this unusual sympathy was clothed. "My pain is not very great," he replied, affably, "& I think has been slightly alleviated thanks to Dr. W. I hope soon to be released from my imprisonment." "You *must* be bored," assented Georgie, then added suddenly as a new thought struck her: "I think you said once you liked . . . you were fond of playing chess. I . . . shall we play a game today?" Lord Breton wondered if the world were upsidedown. "Yes," he said, even more affably, "I was once a good player, & it has always been a favourite pastime of mine. I never proposed it to you, as I understood that—that you had a peculiar aversion to the game." Georgie turned scarlet. "That is nothing," she said, hastily. "I think there is a board in the sitting-room. I will ring." She sent for the board, & the contest immediatly began. How was it that in this new impulse of self-sacrifice Georgie began to lose the lonely weight of her sorrow, & brighten herself in proportion as her efforts dispersed Lord Breton's moody dull-

ness? They were both good players, but Georgie being the
quicker-witted would have won had her tact not shewn her
that she could please Lord Breton better by allowing herself
to be defeated. It was quite late when the game ended, & Georgie had absolutely forgotten her drive; but her husband had
not. "Surely you are going out today, Georgina?" he said. "You
should have gone earlier, indeed. I fear I unintentionally detained you . . ." "Not at all!" she returned, promptly. "I had
not meant to go." "Nevertheless you should take advantage of
the favourable weather. It is not yet too late." "I had rather
stay here, please," said Georgie, but Lord Breton would not
hear of it. He ordered the carriage, & she went up to dress with
a lighter heart than she carried for many a day. As she came
down again, some impulse made her enter her husband's room.
"There is nothing I can do for you in the town?" she asked.
"No, nothing at all, nothing at all," returned Lord Breton in
a gratified voice. "Be careful of the evening air. You are well-
wrapped?" "Oh, yes," she said, lingering. "I shall not be long
gone. Goodbye." "Goodbye." She took a short drive in the
mild Spring air, & came back, strengthened & freshened, before sundown. Strangely enough, there was no one to help her
from the carriage but Sidenham, who always accompanied her;
& in the hall she was met by her physician. A sudden fore-
boding rushed through her mind as she saw him coming
towards her. "What is it?" she said faintly. He gave his arm &
led her quietly into the empty salon. "Sit down, Lady Breton.
Compose yourself, for Heaven's sake," he said. "Lord Breton
is—very ill." She looked at him in a dazed way. "I—I don't
think I understand," she gasped. "Your husband is very dangerously ill," said the physician again. "How can that be? He

was much better when I went out—tell me, tell me!" Sidenham had brought a glass of wine, which she swallowed hurriedly at a sign from the doctor. "Now tell me," she repeated, wildly. "My dear Lady Breton, try to quiet yourself. You say he seemed better—in better spirits—when you went out?" "Yes—I thought so." "So his servant tells me," the physician continued gently. "He said he had not seen his master in such good spirits since he came to Nice.—Compose yourself—Take some more wine. —Half an hour ago I was sent for—" he paused, & in that pause she snatched at the truth he was trying gently to postpone. "He is dead?" she whispered. "Tell me at once. I am calm." "He has been taken from us," the physician answered, his voice tremulous with emotion. "Taken from us without suffering, thank God! His servant went into his room & found him . . . dead. I was sent for at once." "Go on," said Georgie, in a low voice, fixing her tearless eyes on his earnest, pitying face. "I can hear all. He died without . . . pain?" "Entirely. Nothing could have been more sudden or painless." For a little while neither spoke; then Georgie rose suddenly. "Take me to him," she said, in the same calm voice. "Take me, please." "Can you bear it— so soon, Lady Breton?" "Take me," she repeated. "I told him I would come back soon!" She put her hand on the doctor's arm, & he led her out across the hall in silence; but at the door of her husband's room she fainted suddenly, & fell back as she had done at Lochiel House. They carried her up to her room, & it was long before her consciousness could be restored. When she was roused from her stupour it changed into wild fever & delirium, & for nearly a week after Lord Breton's sad & quiet funeral, she lay raving and moaning on her darkened bed. The fever was quieted at last, but she was terribly weakened & even when her mind returned scarcely realized that she had entered into the first days of her widowhood. It was talked of all over Nice, how the old English peer, Lord Breton of Lowood, had been carried off suddenly by the gout, while his wife was out driving; how rich & haughty he was; & how she, poor young creature, delicate, bright & beautiful, & just 21, had been left there in the sunny Mediterranean town, far from friends & home, with no one but her physician & her servants to care for her or to comfort her—had been left there—alone. But perhaps no one quite guessed all the peculiar bitterness that those words contained when, with her returning consciousness they dawned upon Georgie—"left alone."

Chap. XV.   A Summons.

"Could ye come back to me, Douglas, Douglas,
  In the old likeness that I knew!" *Miss Mulock*: "Douglas."

LORD BRETON DIED early in March; & it was three weeks later
that Guy Hastings, returning from a certain eventful visit to
Villa Doria-Pamfili which I have recorded in a previous chapter, found awaiting him at his studio a black-bordered letter
with a Nice postmark. If he had not recognized the writing,
this post-mark would have told him in an instant that it was
from Georgie; for though all intercourse had ceased between
them he had heard through some English friends that she was
passing the Winter at Nice. The black edge & black seal of the
envelope, united to the well-known manuscript, were a deep
shock; & it was several minutes before he could compose himself sufficiently to read the letter.

*"Nice, March ____ th—Dear Guy, I should never venture to
write this if I did not feel sure that I shall not live very long.
Since Lord Breton's death I have been much worse, they say;
but I only know that my heart is breaking, & that I must see
you once for goodbye. If you can forgive all the wrong I have
done you—what bitter suffering it has brought me since!—
come to me as soon as possible. Georgie."*

Hastings could scarcely read the end of the few, trembling lines for the tears that blinded him. Those heart-broken, pleading words seemed to melt away in an instant all the barriers of disappointment & wounded pride, & to wake up the old estranged love that was after all not dead—but sleeping! He scarcely noticed the mention of Lord Breton's death, which reached him now for the first time—he only felt that Georgie was dying, that she had been unhappy & that she loved him still. Then there came a rebellious cry against the fate that reunited them only to part once more. Why must she die when a new promise of brightness was breaking through the storm of life? Why must she die when he was there once more to shield & cherish her as he had dreamed long ago? She should not die! Life must revive with reviving happiness, & the shadow of death wane in the sunrise of their joy. So he raved, pacing his lonely studio, through the long hours of the evening until in the midst of the incoherent flood of thought that overwhelmed him, there flashed suddenly the harsh reality that he had for the moment lost. What if Georgie lived? *He* was not free! How the self-delusion, the hasty mistake of that day, started up cruelly before him in this new light. It was he, then, who had been unfaithful & impatient, & she who had loved on through all, to this cruel end. Thus he reproached himself, as the hopeless cloud of grief closed around him once more. I know not what wild temptations hurried through his mind in that terrible night's struggle. A faint fore-hint of dawn was climbing the gray Orient when at last he threw himself on his bed to seize a few hours sleep before he brought the resolutions of this night into action. He had decided that come what would, he must see Georgie at once—even though it were for the last time, & only to return into the deeper desolation which his error had brought upon him. In this last revolution of feeling he had almost entirely lost sight of the fact that Georgie was dying, & that even in the case of his being free, their parting was inevitable. It seemed to him now that his madness (as he called it in his hopeless self-reproach) had alone exiled him from a renewed life of love & peace with the girl of his heart. He had forgotten, in the whirl of despairing grief, that the shadow of the Angel of Death fell sternly between him & Georgie. When after a short, unrestful sleep he rose & dressed, the morning sun was high over Rome; & he found he had no time to lose if he should attempt to start for Civita Vecchia by the early train. He would not breakfast, but thinking that the early air might freshen him for his long journey, walked immediatly to the Grahams' apartment. He had meant to ask for Mr. Graham, but when he reached the door his heart failed, & he merely told the servant he would not disturb him. Taking one of his cards, he wrote on it hurriedly in pencil: "I am called suddenly to Nice for a few days. Cannot tell when I will be back. Start this morning via Civita Vecchia." He left this for Madeline, knowing that any more elaborate explanation of the object of his journey would be useless; & an hour later he was on his way to Civita Vecchia to meet a steamer to Genoa. The weary, interminable hours drew slowly towards the night; but it seemed to Hastings that the sad journey would never come to an end. When he reached Nice the next morning after a day & a night of steady travel, the strain of thought & fatigue had been so great that he was scarcely conscious of his surroundings, & having driven to the nearest Hôtel went at once up to his room to rest, if indeed rest were possible. A blinding headache had come on, & he was glad to lie on the bed with his windows darkened until the afternoon. He had almost lost the power of thinking now; a dull, heavy weight of anguish seemed to press down destroying all other sensation. When at last he felt strong enough to rouse himself, he rang for a servant & enquired for Lady Breton's villa in the hope that someone in the Hôtel might direct him thither—for poor Georgie, in her hasty note, had forgotten to give her address. Lord Breton's death had made too much noise in Nice for his residence to remain unknown; but Guy, not feeling as well as he had fancied, sat down & wrote a few lines asking when he should find Georgie prepared for him—& despatched these by the servant. It was a great relief when, about an hour later, a note was brought back in the meek, ladylike handwriting of Mrs. Rivers, who had of course joined her daughter on Lord Breton's death. *Dear Guy*, it ran,

We think our darling Georgie is a little better today, but not strong enough to see you. If she is no worse tomorrow, can you come in the afternoon at about four o'clock? This is a time of great anxiety for us all, which I am sure you must share. My poor child longs to see you. Your loving Cousin, M.A. Rivers.

Hastings scarcely knew how that miserable day passed. He had intended writing to Mr. Graham, but he had lost all power of self-direction, & the one absorbing thought that pressed upon him drowned every lesser duty in its vortex of hopeless pain. Early the next morning he sent to the Villa to enquire after Georgie, & word was brought that my lady was no worse, so that a faint hope began to buoy him up as the hours crept on towards the time appointed for their meeting. His agitation was too intense for outward expression, & he was quite calm when at four o'clock he started out on foot through the sunny streets. It was not a long way to the white villa in its fragrant rose-garden; & before long a servant dressed in black had ushered him into the cool salon where a slight, pink-eyed personage in heavier black than of old, came tearfully forward to meet him. "She will be so glad to see you, Guy," wept poor Mrs. Rivers. "She said you were to come at once. Are you ready? This is the way."

Chap. XVI.   Too Late.

"Tis better to have loved & lost
Than never to have loved at all." *Tennyson.* In Memoriam.

GUY FOLLOWED MRS. RIVERS in silence as she led the way across the polished hall & up a short flight of stairs. Leaving him a moment in a small, sunny boudoir bright with pictures & flowers, she went on into an inner room where there was a faint sound of voices. Returning a moment later, she came up & laid an appealing hand of his arm. "You will be careful, dear Guy, not to agitate her? She is so easily excited, so weak, poor darling! Come now." She threw the door open, standing back for him to enter the room, & then closed it softly upon him. It was a large room, with two windows through which the mellow afternoon sunlight streamed; & beside one of these windows, in a deep, cushioned arm-chair Georgie sat with a pale, expectant face. So fragile, so sad & white she looked that he scarcely knew her as he crossed the threshold; then she held out her thin little hand & called softly: "Guy!" It was the old voice; that at least had not changed! He came forward almost blindly, & felt his hand grasped in the soft, trembling fingers on which his parting kiss had fallen more than a year ago. He could not speak at first, & she too was silent; both lost in the intensity of their emotion. "Sit down beside me," she said at last, still clasping his hand gently; & then he looked up again

& met the wide, burning hazel eyes brimmed with tears. "Oh, Guy," she cried, "I never thought to see you again. Have you come to forgive me?" "Do not talk of that," he answered with an effort. "Only tell me that you are stronger, that you will be well soon." She shook her head quietly. "I cannot tell you that; & I *must* tell you how I have suffered through my folly—my wicked folly." Her tears were falling softly, but she made no attempt to hide them. "I think," she went on, still holding Guy's hand, "that the thought—which pursued me always & everywhere—of the wrong I did you, has killed me. When I look back at the hours of shame & suffering I have passed, I almost wonder I lived through them—I almost feel glad to die! Surely, surely there never was so wicked & miserable a creature in the world—I shudder at the mere thought of my hard, silly selfishness." She paused, her voice broken by a sob; then hurried on, as if to relieve herself of a great weight. "Oh, Guy, it would not have been so bad if all this time I had not—cared; but I did. There was no one like you—no one with whom I could feel really happy as with you. Then I thought I would drown all these sad recollections by going into society; but under all the gayety & the noise, Guy, my heart ached—ached so cruelly! Listen a moment longer. When I thought how you must despise me & hate me, I felt like killing myself. I seemed to have been such a traitor to you, although you were the only man I ever loved! I gave up all thought of seeing you again until—until I heard them say I was dying, & then I got courage, remembering how tender & how generous you always were—& as I lay there after the fever left me, I could think nothing but: 'I must see Guy, I must be forgiven,' over & over again." Her voice failed again, & she leaned back among her cushions.

"And you came," she continued, presently, "you came though I had wronged you & insulted you and—and deserved nothing but your contempt. You have come to forgive me!" "Hush, dearest," Guy answered, struggling to master his voice, "try to forget everything that is past. Let us be happy—for a little while." "Oh, I am so happy," she cried; "perhaps, after all, then, you did not think of me quite so hardly—as I deserved. Perhaps—you understood a little—you felt sorry—" "My dearest," he answered, passionately; "I did more; I—loved you." A new light seemed to flash over her face; he could feel the hand that clasped his tighten & tremble. "Don't—don't," she gasped, in a voice full of pain, "it can't be true—don't try to love me—I—I only meant to be forgiven." "Forgiven!" said Guy, with a sudden bitterness, "it is I who need to be forgiven, if there is forgiveness in Heaven or earth for such folly & madness as have been mine! Oh, Georgie darling, I think I have been in a horrible dream." Startled by the sudden wildness of his words, Georgie lifted her eyes full of sorrowful questioning to his. "What is it, Guy? Are we all to be unhappy?" And then, in a few, broken words of shame & self-reproach, he told her how when all the hope & sacredness of life was slipping from him, he had met Madeline, & thinking that such a pure presence might hallow his days, & recall him from the reckless path to which despair had beckoned him, had asked her to be his wife. When he ended, Georgie sat quite still, a grave pity shining in the eyes that seemed too large for her little, wasted face. "I am so glad, Guy," she said, in her sweet, tremulous tone, still clasping his hand; "so glad that I may die without that dreadful thought of having spoiled your life as well as my own. Oh, Guy, I am quite happy now! I am sure she must

be good & gentle, because you are fond of her; & I am sure
she will be a good wife to you, because—no one could help it."
She paused a moment, but he could not trust himself to speak,
& gathering strength, she went on with touching earnestness,
"Guy, you will be good to her, will you not? And you will
make her home pleasant, & forget everything that is gone for
her sake? And kiss her, Guy, on her wedding-day, from some
one who calls herself her sister. Do you promise?" "Anything,
dearest girl," he answered, brokenly. She smiled; one of those
rare, brilliant smiles that to his tear-dimmed eyes made her
face as the face of an Angel. "My own brave Guy," she whispered. "And you will go back to your painting, & your work—
& when I am dead, no one will say 'She ruined his life.' " "They
will say, dearest, that if forgiving love & tenderness could wash
out his folly, when he thought that nothing but despair was
left in life, she did so as no one else could." "Hush, Guy, hush,"
she faltered, as he kissed the trembling hand laid on his own,
"you pain me. I do not deserve so much. I do not deserve to
die so happy—so unspeakably happy." "To die!" he repeated,
passionately. "Darling, do [not] say that—I had almost forgotten! They said you were better." She shook her head, again
with that sweet, flitting smile. "It is better you should know,
Guy—& indeed all is best! I have not courage to live, if I had
the strength. But you must go back to a braver & a happier life,
& then to die will be like going to sleep with the consciousness
that the day is over, & when I wake there will be . . . no more
sorrow & regrets. . . ." There was a long pause. The clock
ticked steadily; the afternoon sunshine waned, & the sand in
an hour-glass on the table trickled its last grains through to
mark the ended hour. Guy sat clasping the little wasted fingers,

& leaning his face against his hand in the hopeless silence of grief. At last Georgie, bending towards him, spoke, very tenderly & quietly: "Look Guy; the twilight is coming. We must say goodbye." "Goodbye?" he echoed vaguely, only half-startled out of his bitter dream by the strangely calm, low words. "For the last time," Georgie went on, drawing her hand softly away. "Oh, Guy, say again before you go that you forgive me everything—everything." He had risen, dazzled by his tears, & turned to the window that she might not see his white face & quivering lips; he could not answer. "Guy, Guy," she repeated passionately, "you forgive me? Guy, come closer; bend down, so, that I may see your face—for it is growing dark. Say 'I forgive you,' Guy!" "I—forgive you." Once more the old, radiant smile, transfiguring her pale features as health & enjoyment had never done, answered his broken words. "Thank you—that is all I wanted," she whispered, gazing up into the haggard face bent over her. "If you knew, Guy, how happy I am...now...." Silence again. "Now kiss me, Guy, & bid me goodnight." Almost childishly, she held up her little, trembling lips; & stifling back his anguish he stooped & kissed them solemnly. "Guy, goodnight." "Goodnight . . . my Love! my Love!—"

. . . . .

Someone led him gently from the room; & he knew that he had seen the face of his beloved for the last time on earth. The next morning word was brought him that Georgie had passed very quietly with the dawn, "to where, beyond these voices, there is Peace."

Chap. XVII. Afterwards.

"—But who that has loved forgets?" *Old Song.*

FIVE YEARS FRUITFUL in many a silent change, have passed
since the life-chronicle which filled these pages, closed with
Georgie Breton's peaceful death; fruitful in so great changes,
that before parting with the different persons who have filled
our story-world, it is tempting to take one last glance into their
altered lives & households, that we may carry away with us the
memory, not of what they were, but of what they are. The villa
at Nice in which Lord Breton & his young wife died has passed
into other hands; but the story of the old English Lord's death,
followed so soon & so tragically by that of the beautiful milady,
still clings to it, & marks it with a peculiar interest. As for Mrs.
Rivers, on her eldest daughter's death she returned at once to
the seclusion of Holly Lodge, where she spends her time in
tears & retirement, overwhelmed by her crape trimmings,
overwhelmed by the education of her children, & by everything, poor lady, which comes in her way. A distant cousin of
the late Lord Breton's (a grave married man with a large
family) has inherited his title & his estates; & there are three
blooming, marrigeable girls at Lowood; for whom the new
Lord & Lady Breton are continually giving croquet-parties,
dinners & balls in the hope that the eligible young men of the
county may be attracted thither, & discover their charms. Mr.

and Mrs. Graham have come back to England too, & have bought a pretty, well-kept little place not far from London, whose walls are adorned with many foreign works of art, collected during their memorable tour on the continent. The honest couple live very quietly, keeping occasional feast-days when the postman leaves at the door a thick blue envelope with a foreign stamp; an envelope containing a pile of close-written sheets beginning "Darling Mamma & Papa" & ending "Your own loving daughter, Madeline." And with what pride will they shew you a photograph, which was enclosed in one of these very letters, of a little, earnest, bright-eyed man of two or three, on the back of which a loving hand has written "Baby's picture." One more English household calls our attention before we wander back for the last time to Italian skies; a comfortable London house in a pleasant neighbourhood, near all the clubs. Jack Egerton is established there; our Bohemian Jack, who has come into a nice fortune in the course of these last years, & has also met with a pale, melancholy, fascinating French Marquise, who so far disturbed his cherished theories of misogynism, that a very quiet wedding was the result of their intimacy, & who now presides with a tact, a grace, & a dignity of which he may well be proud, at his friendly table. So we leave him; to turn once more before parting, to a familiar, though now a changed scene—the old studio on the third floor of the Roman palazzo, where in the old days, Hastings & Egerton lounged & painted. A Signore Inglese has rented the whole floor now; & that Signore is Guy. The studio is essentially as it was; but the glamour of a woman's presence has cast the charm of order & homelikeness over its picturesque chaos, & the light footsteps of a woman cross & recross the floor as Hastings sit[s] at his easel in the sunshine. For, as will have been divined, Guy has fulfilled Georgie's latest prayer, & for nearly five years Madeline Graham has been his wife. They spend their Winters always in Rome, for the sake at once of Madeline's health & Hastings' art-studies; & there is a younger Guy who is beginning to toddle across the studio floor to his father's knee, guided by a little, blushing velvet-eyed Italian Nurse whom he has been taught to call Teresina. Guy works harder than of old, & is on a fair road to fame. He has not forgotten his old friend & Mentor, Egerton, but I doubt if he will ever accept the constant invitations to England which kind-hearted Jack sends him. For there are certain memories which time cannot kill, & change cannot efface. So Madeline is happy in a sunny, peaceful household; in returning health, & new & pleasant duties; in the most beautiful boy that mother ever sung to sleep or woke with a laughing kiss; & in a husband, who is the soul of grave courtesy & kindness. But Guy Hastings' heart is under the violets on Georgie's grave.

The End.

Contents

The End.

Begun in the Autumn of 1876 at Pencraig, Newport; finished
January 7th 1877 at New York.

Three Reviews

"Fast and Loose—A Novelette" by David Olivieri
(*From* The Saturday Review)

It is a melancholy study of human nature to observe the suicidal passion for novel-writing of a certain numerous class of harmless fanatics who, without having a grain of literary talent or training, avail themselves of the freedom of the press to inundate a long suffering public with yellow-coloured volumes of twaddling romance. Among the latest of these deluded self-murderers we may mention (with peculiar compassion for his case seems indeed desperate) the author of "Fast & Loose," a gentleman(?) revelling in the sumptuous name of David Olivieri—a combination suggesting vividly the statuary in the Groves of Blarney, "both Neptune, Plutarch, & Nicodemus." On first opening the pages of this "novelette," (let us be thankful it is no more) we are impressed with an idea of dashing fastness, & expect to find in a hero named Guy Hastings, who belongs to Swift's Club & has had "a dozen little affaires de coeur," the darling type of the "bold bad man" of modern literature. The very title suggests something desperate. Who is fast? What is loose? Apparently the author's well-meant intention was that everybody & everything should be fast & loose. In the very first chapter, the charming heroine describes herself as "a wicked, fast, flirtatious little pauper—a lazy, luxurious coquette!" Guy is again hopefully mentioned as "belonging to that large class whom anxious mothers call fast," &

we feel a thrill of greedy expectation when we hear that he "lived neither better nor worse than a hundred other young men" belonging to the same class. Furthermore, Guy's friend Egerton informs us that he is "not a parson either & doesn't care to preach"; & on our first introduction to Lord Breton, the peer of the story, we fondly dream to perceive the vestiges of a courtly roué of the old school. Such are the great hopes that Mr. Olivieri raises in the bosoms of his too-confident readers. We prophesy 128 pages of racy trash & are glad to think we shall be wasting our time agreeably. How is it then, that the hero evaporates into a vascillating sentimentalist who, though he is ostentatiously & repeatedly labelled as "going to the Dogs," takes so quiet & respectable a road to that mysterious goal that we have an irrepressible desire to push him on a little faster? How is it that the heroine, who, we are anxiously informed, is the fastest woman in London, does nothing that would have raised a blush on the rigid countenance of an elderly Quakeress? How is it that Lord Breton melts into a harmless gourmet, & Egerton gloomily moralizes, though he so sternly refuses to preach? It is plain, before we are well-launched on this ocean of vice, that Mr. Olivieri's talent does not lie in the painting of publicans & sinners. Nor is he more successful in the angelical contrast which he offers to the heroine's worldliness, in the person of Madeline Graham. If Madeline be Mr. Olivieri's conception of innocence, we no longer have any difficulty in understanding the motives which prompted Herod to the Massacre of the Innocents. Between these two representatives of Virtue & Vice (as Mr. Olivieri understands them) Hastings oscillates gently; until, being thrown over by Vice, he flies for salvation from some rather vague moral danger, to the willing arms of Virtue. But it would be cruel to Mr. Olivieri to take the last gloss from his gingerbread by revealing the intricacies of the thrilling plot which connects the lives of the individuals whose characters we have taken the liberty so frankly to handle. We content ourselves by saying in a sweeping summary, that whatever character Mr. Olivieri hopefully attempts to pourtray, we lose before long all the boundaries of its individuality, & find ourselves towards the welcome last page involved in a chaos of names apparently all seeking their owners. Guy might as well be Madeline, & vice versa. The Pharisees & the publicans (to continue our Biblical figure) sit down at meat together, & when they arise it seems that the mutual contact must have effaced whatever distinctive marks they originally possessed.

From the Pall Mall Budget

... And in concluding our survey of the melancholy band of nonentities which form the dramatis personae of this dolorous tale, our eye rests with pain & astonishment on the multilated, useless, unfinished picture of the Italian peasant-girl Teresina. It is evidently the author's first intention to make the hero fall indiscreetly & ruinously in love with this pretty little negative —but again Mr. Olivieri's unaesthetical morality conquers; he leaves Teresina & Guy intact, & in the end marries both in a lawful & prosaic way. Teresina's marriage is indeed followed by a tragedy of sickness & desertion; but a tragedy evidently concocted by Mr. Olivieri to get the poor girl off his hands & make way for Hastings' third & sickliest goddess, Madeline Graham...

From The Nation

... In short, in such a case, it is false charity to reader & writer to mince matters. The English of it is that every character is a failure, the plot a vacuum, the style spiritless, the dialogue vague, the sentiments weak, & the whole thing a fiasco. Is not —the disgusted reader is forced to ask—is not Mr. Olivieri very, very like a sick-sentimental school-girl who has begun her work with a fierce & bloody resolve to make it as bad as Wilhelm Meister, Consuelo, & "Goodbye Sweetheart" together, & has ended with a blush, & a general erasure of all the naughty words which her modest vocabulary could furnish? ...

Appendixes

"I know how precious is the treasure I have dared to ask for —
I shall try to make myself worthy of her by guarding her more
tenderly than my own life — if indeed you consent"... ...
Madeline turned a shy, appealing glance at Mr Graham as she
stood clinging to her mother. "Eh, Maddy?" said the soft merchant,
goodnaturedly, "what can the old father say, after all? Well — I
don't know how to refuse — we must think, we must think" —
• "Madeline," said Hastings, bending over her, "will you take my
arm to the carriage?" They did not say much as they walked
along in the dying sunset light; but a pleasant sense of
possessorship came over Guy as he felt the shy hand lying on
his arm — & who ~~then~~ can sum up the wealth of Madeline's
silent happiness? — And so they passed through the gates, & the
Spring twilight fell over Villa Doria — Pamfili —
    Chap. XIV   Left Alone.
"Death, like a robber, crept in unaware." Old Play (From the Spanish)
. Three slow weeks of illness followed Georgie's imprudence
at Lochill House; & in September when she began to grow a little
better, she was ordered off to the Mediterranean for the winter. She
scarcely regretted this; the trip in Lord Breton's yacht would be
pleasant, & any change of scene welcome for a time — but as far
as her health was concerned, she cared very little ~~it~~ for its preservation, since life in every phase grew more hopelessly weary day
by day. Favourable winds made their ~~journey~~ short & smooth,

Page 108 of the manuscript of Edith Wharton's *Fast and Loose*.
(Courtesy the Clifton Waller Barrett Collection, the University of
Virginia Library.)

Notes

2.1   "Let woman beware. . . ." From *Lucile*, a novel in verse by Edward Robert Bulwer-Lytton (1831–1891), published under the pseudonym of "Owen Meredith" in 1860. It was criticized for plagiarism (from George Sand's *Lavinia*), its mesmeric metrical form, and its diffuseness. It was nevertheless immensely popular with the general public; it offered escape to the fashionable spas of Germany and the Pyrenees, where the characters—all rich and aristocratic—labor only at love. The galloping rhythm of its anapestic couplets (allegedly Lytton composed most of *Lucile* on horseback) is ludicrously inapt in the serious parts but gives an aphoristic fillip to its moral and satiric commentary. It was a favorite of young ladies in quest of epigrams and moral sentiments to copy into their albums; to its quotability must be attributed part of its success for two generations. Reaching a fifth edition in 1893, it was especially popular in the United States. Its author, known as Robert Lytton (not to be confused with his novelist father, Edward Bulwer, First Lord of Lytton), had a distinguished career as a diplomat. He was viceroy of India when Queen Victoria was proclaimed Empress of India, and for his service in that high post he was created Earl of Lytton.

2.6   "Cornélie." Almost certainly Emelyn Washburn, the

only child of the rector of Calvary Church in New York. The quotation, partially obliterated from having been covered by a tape or a strip of paper, now removed, is probably from Dante's *Inferno*, canto II, line 53, preceding Beatrice's first appearance in the poem: "e donna mi chiamò beata e bella" (A blessed and beautiful lady called me). Six years older than Edith, quick-witted, a lover of music, interested in literature and politics, Emelyn was a stimulating and affectionate friend. Their friendship, in R. W. B. Lewis's view the most valuable Edith was to have with another girl, began in Newport the summer of 1875. The quotation may be a pleasant allusion to the occasions when they read Dante aloud to each other. It may also be interpreted as Edith's tribute to her older friend's devotion and intellectual guidance. Later, Edith Wharton saw her friend in a different light. In "Life and I," an unpublished fragmentary memoir of the 1930s, she expressed the suspicion that in Miss Washburn "there were strong traces of degeneracy" (meaning lesbianism), though she had not realized it at the time. She describes Emelyn as becoming "passionately, morbidly attached to me; & as she was extremely cultivated & a great reader (though not really intelligent) she soon saw that I was starving for mental nourishment, & poured it out upon me in reckless profusion." The only evidence she gives for what may be taken as a lack of intelligence is Emelyn's encouraging her to learn Anglo-Saxon, an accomplishment that gave Edith little satisfaction. In the same memoir, abandoned perhaps for being too unguarded, Edith Wharton said that her acquaintance with Emelyn came about because she had fallen in love with Emelyn's father, a man of about fifty-five; she was about thirteen. Her "consuming passion" for him "raged for three or four years to the exclusion of every other affection." The object of this passion was apparently unaware of it, and Edith's ardor, possibly overstated here, was more aesthetic than erotic: "very sensitive to qualities of intonation, & to beauty of diction," she was enraptured by his "beautiful voice"; "it was ecstasy to me to sit in the dusky shadowy church, & hear him call out: 'What though I have fought with the beasts at Ephesus?' or 'Canst thou loose the sweet influences of the Pleiades?' "

3.4 " ' 'Tis best to be off. . . .' " An Anglicized version of a Scots song, the first verse of which is:

> It's gude to be merry and wise,
> It's gude to be honest and true;
> And afore ye're off wi' the auld love,
> It's best to be on wi' the new.

This is as it appears in *The Songs of England and Scotland* (1835). The last two lines are also quoted in Scott's *The Bride of Lammermoor* (1819) and Trollope's *Barchester Towers* (1855).

11.2 " 'Auld Robin Gray. . . .' " From the ballad of that name by Lady Anne Barnard, written about 1772. This story of a January to May marriage has a happy ending: Auld Robin Gray opportunely dies, but not before blessing his young wife and reuniting her with her first love.

21.20 "Fortunatus." A hero in medieval legend of Eastern origin, Fortunatus possessed an inexhaustible purse.

25.2 " 'Through you, whom once. . . .' " Slightly misquoted from "The Letters," Tennyson, ll. 35–36: "And you, whom I loved so well / Thro' you my life will be accurst."

26.26 "*Swift's Club, Regent St.*" The earlier address, St. James

St., page 17, for Guy's club is more suitable than this one, which must be an error in transcription.

27.15   "with a bust of Pallas." A parodic echo of Poe's "The Raven." Though Egerton does not perch on the "bust of Pallas," his "sharp, short rap at the door of [Guy's] sanctum" and misogynistic pronouncements recall the raven and his "nevermore."

28.19   "Telemachus." An allusion not to Homer's Odyssey but to Fénélon's *The Adventures of Telemachus*, in which the hero, cautioned by Mentor, resists Calypso's advances. Mentor not only counsels flight (as Egerton does to Guy) to escape the temptress, but finally pushes Telemachus from a rock into the sea, making return to the island rather difficult.

29.2   " 'Every woman is at heart a rake'!" From *Moral Epistles*, "Epistle to a Lady," l. 216: "Men, some to bus'ness, some to pleasure take; / But ev'ry woman is at heart a rake."

31.6   "Salvandy." Narcisse Achille Salvandy (1795–1856), a conservative French statesman and author of *Revolution and the Revolutionaries* (1830).

32.3   "Bismarck-coloured." Short for bismarck-brown, a dull yellowish brown color. Its etymology unknown, it probably derives from Prince Otto von Bismarck (1815–1898). More specifically, it may come from the color of the uniforms worn by German troops in the Franco-Prussian War. It was an innovation for soldiers to wear uniforms that blended into the terrain.

33.19   "Miss Ingelow." Jean Ingelow (1820–1897), English poet and children's writer, is now best remembered for her children's book *Mopsa the Fairy* (1869). In her own day her verse, blending Wordsworth with Tennyson, was widely read, especially in the United States.

37.2   " 'I & he, Brothers in art.' " From "The Gardener's Daughter: or, the Pictures," ll. 3–4.

45.2   " 'Oh, to be England. . . .' " The opening lines of "Home Thoughts from Abroad," in Browning's *Dramatic Lyrics*.

54.25–26   " 'The roses had shuddered. . . .' " From chapter 13, *The History of Henry Esmond*; in full the sentence is "The roses had shuddered out of her cheeks; her eyes were glaring; she looked quite old."

57.2   " 'The lady, in truth, was young. . . .' " This refers to Mathilda, Madeline's counterpart in *Lucile* (part 2, canto 2, stanza 3).

60.11   " 'The Gardener's Daughter.' " In this poem by Tennyson the speaker, a painter like Guy, falls in love with the gardener's golden-haired daughter Rose at first sight when he sees her tending her flowers.

64.2   " 'Through those days. . . .' " This quotation and others attributed to old plays or songs suggest that where memory failed, invention stepped in—a not uncommon nineteenth-century practice with epigraphs. Although variants of these quotations are to be found in dictionaries of proverbs and quotations, I have been unable to trace exact sources, not even in the plays Edith Jones read or in Robert Chambers's *Cyclopaedia of English Literature*, a compilation of British authors from Anglo-Saxon times to her present, which was her basic text for her English studies.

71.2   " 'Adieu, bal, plaisir, amour. . . .' " Probably from a work by the French dramatist Germain Delavigne (1790–1868), known for his vaudevilles, comedies, and libretti.

79.2   " 'When pain & anguish. . . .' " From canto 6, stanza 30, of *Marmion*. The preceding lines are:

O, Woman! in our hours of ease,
Uncertain, coy, and hard to please,
And variable as the shade
By the light quivering aspen made;

88.1-2 "Robert Spencer's bright words." William Robert Spencer (1769–1834) was a translator and fashionable author of light verse.

99.2 " 'Could ye come back. . . .' " From the poem "Too Late," by Dinah Maria Mulock [Craik] (1826–1887), British novelist, poet, and children's writer. Her rags-to-riches novel *John Halifax, Gentleman* (1856) was a bestseller; it is now only a footnote in histories of Victorian novels of social reform. Her poetry proved to be even more ephemeral. Unlike Georgie the fickle young lady in this poem is not reconciled with her lover in this world; she remorsefully begs him to "drop forgiveness from heaven like dew."

108.27 " 'to where, beyond these voices. . . .' " The last line of Tennyson's "Guinevere," from *Idylls of the King.*

121.8 " 'Goodbye Sweetheart.' " A novel (1872) by the British author Rhoda Broughton (1840–1920). As her books in this period of high Victorian prudishness were considered bold and improper reading for young ladies, the yoking of this novel with Sand's and Goethe's would not have seemed as incongruous then as it does to us now. The titles of some of her most popular works indicate the nature of her appeal to her contemporaries: *Cometh Up as a Flower, An Autobiography* (1867), *Not Wisely But Too Well* (1867), *Doctor Cupid* (1886), and *Alas! A Novel* (1890).

Revisions

3.9   Holly] *above deleted* 'Pine'

5.25   still] *followed by deleted* 'abou'

7.18   on] *over erased* 'onto'

8.7   if] *followed by deleted* 'my'

8.11   shopping] *above deleted* 'marketing'

8.16   First] *over erased* 'Lord B'

14.19   opposite] *comma inserted and followed by deleted* '& leaned'

18.3   emotions] *preceded by deleted* 'refle'

18.7   member] *preceded by deleted* 'man in'

19.3   them] *preceded by deleted* 'it'

20.4   people] *preceded by deleted* 'men'

20.7   talent] *followed by deleted* 'a love of'

20.8   bewitching] *preceded by erased* 'fine'

21.10   was leaving] *preceded by deleted* 'turned away'

22.11   woes] *interlined above deleted* 'himself'

22.22   glared] *interlined above deleted* 'stared'

23.4   His] *preceded by deleted* 'the'

23.8   slowly] *interlined above deleted* 'deliberately'

23.10   we were] *interlined above deleted* 'she was'

24.11   kindly] *interlined above deleted* 'unutterable'

25.7   in] *preceded by deleted* 'fr'

25.12   Georgie] *preceded by deleted* 'She'

25.23   for] *interlined above deleted* 'but'

27.4   apartment] *interlined above deleted* 'room'

27.9   in] *preceded by deleted* 'at'

28.14   pitied] *preceded by deleted* 'sym' *and followed by deleted* 'his friend' *and* '[Guy]'s sorrow'

28.17   unbelieving] 'un' *interlined above deleted* 'mis'

28.25   Egerton] *preceded by deleted* 'his friend Jack sharply; but'

28.30   the same] *preceded by deleted* 'like that'

30.6   four] *interlined above deleted* 'three'

31.5   needed] *preceded by deleted* 'it tak'

31.13   A] *over partially erased* 'Two'

32.7   rolled] *preceded by deleted* 'passed'

32.23   passing] *preceded by deleted* 'overrated pleasures'

33.2   out] *preceded by deleted* 'anything else'

33.18   Altogether] *preceded by deleted* 'never'

33.19   Ingelow] *preceded by deleted* 'Je'

34.10   Is] *preceded by deleted* 'Has the'

35.24   at] *preceded by deleted* 'for'

36.8   heavy] *preceded by deleted* 'the'

37.16   made] *interlined above deleted* 'gave'

38.10   hinted] *preceded by deleted* 'obs'

38.13   but] *preceded by deleted* 'sublimely,'

39.11   16] *superimposed on* '17'

40.29   palette] *preceded by deleted* 'colours'

41.21   take] *preceded by deleted* 'wou'

42.1   met] *preceded by deleted* 'spot'

42.26   we] *preceded by deleted* 'you will'

43.6   do] *interlined above deleted* 'commit'

48.4   Hebe's] *preceded by deleted* 'nymph's'

48.10   &] *followed by deleted* 'made'

49.16   reveal] *preceded by deleted* 'disclose'

50.8   bosom] *interlined above deleted* 'throat & neck'

50.23   with] *preceded by deleted* 'beside a'

51.22 orders] *preceded by* 'obliges to'
52.22 in] *preceded by deleted* 'as she'
53.14 & it] *preceded by deleted* 'that'
55.9 thoroughly] *preceded by deleted* 'not'
58.8 whatever] *preceded by deleted* 'all'
58.9 April] *interlined above and between* 'one' *and* 'morning'
58.11 Giovanni] *preceded by deleted* 'Baptis'
58.14 went] *preceded by deleted* 'ga'
58.16 wrote to] *interlined above deleted* 'told'
58.18 &] *followed by deleted* 'only'
59.1 parasol.] *followed by deleted* 'on the'
59.18 fashionable] *interlined above deleted* 'lesser'
60.4 woman-kind] *preceded by deleted* 'human-natu'
60.6 among . . . classes] *interlined above and after* 'beauty.'
61.8 smile.] *followed by deleted* 'half holding out her hand.'
61.14 Mr. Graham] *interlined above deleted* 'her father'
61.14 Madeline] *interlined above deleted* 'she'
61.24 apartments] *interlined above deleted* 'rooms'
62.9 an hour] *preceded by deleted* 'half'
66.25 perfectly] *interlined above deleted* 'quite'
67.20 fair] *preceded by deleted* 'sweet'
68.3 When] *preceded by deleted* 'But'
68.25 weary] *preceded by deleted* 'sadness'
69.3 days were] *interlined and over deleted* 'life was'
72.14 had] *interlined above deleted* 'might'
72.28 place] *preceded by deleted* 'affection she had'
74.24 expressively] *preceded by deleted* 'obser'
74.29 continually] *interlined above deleted* 'with everyone'
75.21 on the threshold] *interlined above with caret*
75.23 from] *interlined above deleted* 'through'
75.26 ceiling] *preceded by deleted* 'roof'
76.2 as] *preceded by deleted* 'like th'

76.9 specimens] *preceded by deleted* 'rare'

76.17 crowded] *preceded by deleted* 'qu'

76.18 cannot] *preceded by deleted* 'do'

77.7 wooed] *preceded by deleted* 'met'

77.24 but] *preceded by deleted* 'or get'

78.11 suffering] *preceded by deleted* 'face &'

78.17 a] *written over deleted* 'an' *and followed by deleted* 'unused'

78.18 his] *preceded by deleted* 'the'

79.24 given in] *deleted* 'to' *interlined above; followed by deleted* 'the big lonely studio' *with* 'big' *interlined above* 'lonely'

80.1 honour] *followed by deleted* 'in the big studio in the Via'

80.4 grew] *preceded by deleted* 'dis'

80.5–6 discover] *preceded by deleted* 'fas'

80.18 &] *preceded by deleted* 'to meet'

80.23 at] *preceded by deleted* 'he'

80.25 against a] *followed by deleted* 'the wall'; 'a' *interlined above* 'the'

80.27 &] *preceded by deleted* '& as he'

81.28 glancing] *preceded by deleted* 'surprised.'

81.29 maid] *preceded by deleted* 'Engli'

82.26 they] *preceded by deleted* '& seen Teresina laid on a bed'

83.15 shawls] *preceded by deleted* 'clo'

83.18 suffering] *interlined above deleted* 'grief'

84.5 have] *preceded by deleted* 'are'

84.14 harsh] *preceded by deleted* 'cr'

84.17 Teresina] *preceded by deleted* 'at last'

84.28 would] *preceded by deleted* 'ca'

85.8 Few] *preceded by deleted* 'Indeed,'

85.11 shy] *interlined above deleted* 'quiet'

87.26 & then] *interlined above deleted* 'sitt'

88.8 &] *preceded by deleted* 'with her'

88.28 he] *preceded by deleted* 'talking shyly'

89.9 I] *preceded by deleted* ' "Look," said'

90.5 in] *preceded by deleted* 'presently'

90.24 burning] *preceded by deleted* 'flaming'

91.17 weeping] *preceded by deleted* 'hiding'

92.2 can] *preceded by deleted* 'knows'

93.12 passage] *interlined above deleted* 'journey'

93.13 poorly] *preceded by deleted* 'feeb'

93.18 several] *interlined above deleted* 'a'

94.4 did not] *interlined above deleted* 'never'; 'red' *deleted from* 'occurred'

94.5 March] *interlined with caret above* 'day'

94.17 failed] *preceded by deleted* 'not'

94.23 cheek] *preceded by deleted* 'eyes'

94.26 harmonious] *preceded by deleted* 'mysterious'

94.26 the ends] 'the' *interlined above deleted* 'her'

94.28 cherished—] *followed by deleted* 'she s'

95.14 this] *superimposed on partially deleted* 'these'

95.14 sympathy] *preceded by deleted* 'words were'

97.10 truth] *preceded by deleted* 'realit'

97.26 &] *preceded by deleted* '& would hav'

97.28 nearly] *preceded by deleted* 'more'

98.5 & haughty] *preceded by deleted* 'he was &'

100.17 until in] *interlined with caret above deleted* 'In'

100.26 A] *preceded by deleted* 'The dawn'

102.2 bed] *preceded by deleted* 'lounge b'

102.11 as . . . fancied] *interlined above deleted* 'able to take a step,'

102.19 afternoon] *interlined above deleted* 'morning'

102.19   four] *preceded by deleted* 'twelve o'clock'

102.25   absorbing] *revised from* 'absorption' *by deleting* 'ption'
          and adding 'bing'

104.20   &] *preceded by deleted* 'to'

105.19   Then] *preceded by deleted* 'You may'

105.29   Guy] *preceded by deleted* 'him'

106.12   voice] *preceded by deleted* 'low'

106.28   still] *preceded by deleted* 'laying her'

107.17   trembling] *preceded by deleted* 'little,'

111.3   nearly five] *interlined above deleted* 'four'

111.9   He] *preceded by deleted* 'but'

111.13   efface] *preceded by deleted* 'alter'

118.28   representatives] *preceded by deleted* 'heroes'

119.9   a] *preceded by deleted* 'such'

Misspellings

Included here are only words misspelled according to standard nineteenth-century British practice. Some of the spellings reproduced in the text, such as "despatch," "imbittered," "chesnut" and "bridemaid," were alternate usages according to the *OED*.

4.23	gallopping	53.24	developped
8.4	booh-hooing	60.22	developped
17.11	masculiness	95.27	immediatly
32.1	bouyantly	101.15	immediatly
42.5	elavation	109.21	marrigeable
47.25	roomfull	118.11	vascillating
51.11	quarré		

This first printing of *Fast and Loose*
is limited to an *édition de tête* of 26 copies
in extra binding and lettered A to Z
and 724 copies for the trade.

———————

This edition was composed and printed by
Heritage Printers, Inc., Charlotte, N. C.,
and bound by The Delmar Company.
The type is Garamond
and the paper is Mohawk Superfine.
Design is by Edward G. Foss.